THE CHRISTMAS PRESENT

GRAZIA DELEDDA

THE CHRISTMAS PRESENT
(AND OTHER STORIES)

translated and with an introduction
by
Graham Anderson

Dedalus

Supported using public funding by
**ARTS COUNCIL
ENGLAND**

Published in the UK by Dedalus Limited
24-26, St Judith's Lane, Sawtry, Cambs, PE28 5XE
info@dedalusbooks.com
www.dedalusbooks.com

ISBN printed book   978 1 915568 16 8
ISBN ebook   978 1 915568 36 6

Dedalus is distributed in the USA & Canada by SCB Distributors
15608 South New Century Drive, Gardena, CA 90248
info@scbdistributors.com   www.scbdistributors.com

Dedalus is distributed in Australia by Peribo Pty Ltd
58, Beaumont Road, Mount Kuring-gai, N.S.W. 2080
info@peribo.com.au   www.peribo.com.au

First published in Italy in 1930
First published by Dedalus in 2023

Printed and bound in the UK by Clays Elcograf, S.p.A.
Typeset by Marie Lane

THE AUTHOR

GRAZIA DELEDDA

Grazia Deledda was born in 1871 in Nuoro, Sardinia. The street where she was born has been renamed after her, via Grazia Deledda. She finished her formal education at age eleven. She published her first short story when she was sixteen and her first novel, *Stella D'Oriente* in 1890 in a Sardinian newspaper when she was nineteen. She left Nuoro for the first time in 1899 and settled in Cagliari, the principal city of Sardinia where she met the civil servant Palmiro Madesani whom she married in 1900. They then moved to Rome.

Grazia Deledda wrote her best work between 1903-1920 and established an international reputation as a novelist. Nearly all of her work in this period was set in Sardinia. She published *Elias Portolu* in 1903, *La Madre* in 1920 and won the Nobel Prize for Literature in 1926. She died in 1936 and was buried in the church of Madonna della Solitudine in Nuoro, near to where she was born.

THE TRANSLATOR

GRAHAM ANDERSON

Graham Anderson was born in London. After reading French and Italian at Cambridge, he worked on the book pages of *City Limits* and reviewed fiction for *The Independent* and *The Sunday Telegraph*. As a translator, he has developed versions of French plays, both classic and contemporary, for the NT and the Gate Theatre, with performances both here and in the USA. Publications include *The Figaro Plays* by Beaumarchais and *A Flea in her Ear* by Feydeau.

His translations for Dedalus include *Sappho* by Alphonse Daudet, *Chasing the Dream* and *A Woman's Affair* by Liane de Pougy, *This was the Man (Lui)* by Louise Colet and *This Woman, This Man (Elle et Lui)* by George Sand. He has also translated Grazia Deledda's short story collections *The Queen of Darkness* and *The Christmas Present*. He is currently translating *Marianna Sirca* by Grazia Deledda for Dedalus.

His own short fiction has won or been shortlisted for three literary prizes. He is married and lives in Oxfordshire.

CONTENTS

Introduction

By 1930, when *The Christmas Present* was published, Grazia Deledda had written fifty books, mostly novels, and, in 1926, been awarded the Nobel Prize for Literature (collected at a ceremony in Stockholm the following year). She was only the second woman to receive the honour. Her output may have been prolific but the journey to such recognition had been a long one.

It began in Sardinia, in the hill town of Nuoro, where Deledda was born in September 1871. For almost thirty years the island, and the Nouro district in particular, had been her only world, and it was its inhabitants, their customs, characters and concerns that became the subject of the greater part of her work.

Sardinia had always been distinct from mainland Italy. It had its own language, Sard, and Deledda's mother neither read nor wrote Italian. Grazia herself, after five years of elementary schooling, needed to take lessons from an Italian tutor before she felt competent to advance her ambition to be a writer. It was an unusual ambition, especially for a young woman, even though her family was well-to-do by Nuorese standards. She was the fifth of seven children. Two older brothers received a full education, and her father, trained as a lawyer, was an active local businessman and owner of a number of parcels of farming land. The majority of the population, however, were humble agricultural workers, shepherds or tenant farmers. The women stayed at home. Religious duties and ancient customs were strictly observed. Inter-family feuds had the ferocity of an older civilisation and bandits still lived in the hills.

Grazia Deledda absorbed all of this, the saint's day feasts, the rural festivals, the domestic, social and religious rituals, the Sardinian legends and folk tales. Her schooling gave her a taste for reading and after her formal education (she had added an extra year to the statutory four) she had access to the library of her uncle, a priest, and the Italian tutor's books. In her teenage years she began to write her own stories and poems. A few were published in local journals. She wrote busily to editors both in Cagliari and on the mainland. *L'ultima moda*, a Rome-based fashion magazine, accepted some of her early stories. But most of her young womanhood was spent at home, in the company of her mother, her two younger sisters, the family's servants and the many visitors who came to the house to seek her father's advice and help on various legal and financial matters.

A number of romantically-flavoured short novels, and stories describing the struggles of the island's poor, appeared throughout the 1890s. In 1896 her novel *La via del male (The Way of Evil)* received a long and considered review from the respected writer and critic Luigi Capuana, and it seemed that Deledda's literary ambitions might yet be realised. But the restrictions of life on Sardinia had for some years been becoming too oppressive. Few in Nuoro, even among her own family, appreciated her attempt to forge a literary career. She yearned for a wider life, for a move to mainland Italy, for the chance to live in Rome itself. The chance came when, in 1899, she met Palmiro Madesani, a civil servant in Cagliari, and married him in January 1900. By the middle of March that same year, Deledda had used her by now wider contacts to engineer for him a transfer to a post in the Finance Ministry in the capital, and her new life had begun.

It could be said that at this point her serious literary career began too, for it was in 1900 that the novel which became her first real success, *Elias Portolu*, appeared. It brought her name into the public domain and is still regarded as one of her key works, enshrining as it does nearly all her major themes. Elias Portolu has been serving a prison sentence on the mainland. On his return to his native Sardinia he rejoins his family, only to have the misfortune to fall in love with his brother's fiancée. Stricken by conscience and unable to take the bold and cruel step of claiming her for himself, he changes course entirely to become a priest. When the brother and fiancée die, Elias is torn between grief and the satisfaction of having denied himself what would have been a forbidden love. The battle between desire and social constraint, the indecisive anguish of the central character, the sense of lives left unfulfilled: these are constant subjects in Deledda's work. No less powerful are the evocations of place, of nature and of the joys and miseries of ordinary people's lives in the tough Nuoro countryside.

Further novels quickly followed, among them *Il vecchio della montagna* (*The Old Man of the Mountain*, 1900), *Cenere* (*Ashes*, 1904), *L'edera* (*The Ivy*, 1908). Over the next quarter-century, Deledda published at the rate of a book each year, producing the distinctive body of work that was to lead to her nomination for the Nobel Prize. *Nel deserto* (*In the Desert*, 1911), for example, tells the story of a woman who moves to Rome, falls in love, but is unable to unshackle herself from the repressions of her Sardinian upbringing. *Canne al vento* (*Reeds in the Wind*, 1913), centres on an elderly servant to two sisters and the buried scandal that undermines their lives. Deledda claimed in later life that *Canne al vento* was her own personal favourite among her thirty-three novels, and it has certainly been one of the most popular. *Marianna Sirca* (1915) deals with a proud and repressed woman's infatuation for a Sardinian bandit. *La madre* (*The Mother*, 1920) is held in high regard by the critics for its intensity of focus: a triangle in which a peasant mother who has taken pride in encouraging her son to become a priest is horrified when the son and a young woman of his parish fall in love. She cannot deny the son his right to a happy life, but neither can she condone the fall from grace which would follow his abandoning the priesthood.

This powerfully grim book might lead a reader to suppose the author's outlook on life was similarly pessimistic. But, although a private and reserved woman, Grazia Deledda's character had its softer side and she enjoyed many pleasures. She doted on her two sons, born in 1900 and 1904, and had a particular attachment to her niece, Mirella (a delightful portrait of Mirella as a little girl is one of the pieces in the present collection) and immersed herself happily in the cultural opportunities afforded by living in Rome. Her later works became lighter: *Il paese del vento* (*The Land of the Wind*, 1931), *Sole d'estate* (Summer Sun, 1933). She also wrote some two hundred and fifty short stories, many of them the engaging folk tales she heard as a girl in Nuoro. *The Christmas Present* belongs to this phase. Published in 1930, a year that also saw the novel *La casa del poeta* (*The Poet's House*) and a translation of Balzac's *Eugénie Grandet*, *The Christmas Present* brings together seventeen short pieces, some in the mode of the many stories she wrote for children, others charming reminiscences of her girlhood, still others tales of the supernatural and of ancient superstitions. Together they represent a nostalgic and happy recollection of life in the remote Sardinian hills of the late nineteenth century.

After her death in 1936, an unpublished novel was found among her papers. Entitled *Cosima* — one of her own middle names — it is a lively and atmospheric account of its author's first thirty years. It was published posthumously in 1937 and has been translated into English by Martha King, whose full biography, *Grazia Deledda, A Legendary Life*, is recommended to any reader who wishes to learn the story, much of it in her own words, of this unique writer. As her Nobel citation said, the award was made: 'For her idealistically inspired writings which with fine plasticity picture the life of her native island and with depth and sympathy deal with human problems in general.'

D H Lawrence travelled to Sardinia, including Nuoro, in 1921 and his book *Sea and Sardinia* makes fascinating reading for those wishing to understand the still primitive character of Sardinian life in the early part of the twentieth century.

For further reading, M G Steegman's translation of *La madre* is available in a new edition from Dedalus Books. Along with *The Christmas Present*, Dedalus will shortly be publishing a collection of short stories from the beginning of Deledda's career, *La regina delle tenebre* (*The Queen of Darkness*, 1902) and the novel *Marianna Sirca*.

THE CHRISTMAS PRESENT

The five Lobina brothers, all shepherds, left their sheepfolds and pens to return and spend the night of Christmas Eve in the family home.

It was a special festival for them this year, because their only sister was getting engaged to a young man of considerable wealth.

As is often the practice in Sardinia, the young man was to send a present to his bride-to-be, and then go along himself to share the festival with her family.

And the five brothers were particularly anxious to support their sister in order to show the future brother-in-law that while they were not as rich as he was, they were in exchange strong, healthy and as unified amongst themselves as a band of warriors.

They had sent the youngest brother, Felle, on ahead. He was a fine-looking boy of eleven with big gentle eyes and dressed in sheepskins like a miniature Saint John the Baptist. He had a knapsack slung over his shoulder, and in the knapsack was a newly slaughtered piglet destined to serve as their dinner.

The little village was blanketed in snow. The small black houses, huddled against the mountain slope, stood out as if drawn on white cardboard, and the church, built on a terrace supported by boulders and surrounded by trees laden with snow and hung with icicles, looked like one of those fantastical edifices formed by the clouds.

All was silent: it was as if the inhabitants were buried under the snow. In the street leading to his house, Felle saw no marks in the whiteness except the footprints of a woman, and amused himself by carefully stepping into them. The prints stopped at the rough wooden gate to the courtyard that his family shared with another family of shepherds even poorer than themselves. The two lowly dwellings, one in each half of the courtyard, were as alike as two sisters. Smoke rose from each chimney, thin ribbons of light filtered round each door.

Felle whistled to announce his arrival; and at once, in the neighbour's doorway, a little girl appeared, face red with cold and eyes shining with happiness.

'Welcome back, Felle.'

'Oh, Lia!' he called out, returning the greeting and going over to the small entrance porch from which, as well as light, there now drifted wisps of smoke from a large fire burning in the woodstove in the middle of the kitchen. Around the stove were seated Lia's sisters. To keep them in order, the eldest of them, the next one after Felle's friend, was distributing raisins and singing them a little song appropriate to the occasion, a lullaby for the Infant Jesus.

'What have you got there?' Lia asked, touching Felle's knapsack. 'Ah, the little pig. Well, your sister's young man has already sent the serving girl with his present too. You'll all be having a great celebration,' she added with a trace of envy. But then she recovered herself and announced with an arch smile: 'And so shall we!'

Felle tried to ask her what she meant but Lia closed the door in his face, and he crossed the courtyard to enter his own house.

The house was indeed filled with celebratory smells: the smell of honey cake baking in the oven and the smell of sweetmeats made from orange peel and toasted almonds. Such good smells that Felle began to grind his teeth together as if already sinking them into those delicious but still hidden treats.

The sister, tall and slender, was already wearing her feast-day clothes: her bodice a waistcoat of green brocade, her skirt black and red; around her pale face a headscarf of flowered silk; and on her feet, embroidered shoes with tassels. She was as pretty, in a word, as a young fairy. The mother, however, dressed all in black following her recent widowhood and looking pale also, despite her darker complexion and rather haughty demeanour, might have put one in mind of a witch, had it not been for the great softness of her eyes, which resembled Felle's.

The boy meanwhile pulled from his bag the piglet, all red because they had stained its skin with its own blood. And after handing it over to his mother he wanted to see the one sent as

17

a gift by the sister's fiancé. Yes, the fiancé's was bigger, almost a proper pig; but the one he had brought, more tender and with less fat, would certainly be more tasty.

'But if our neighbours only have a few raisins in the house, while we have these two fine animals, what kind of celebrations can they be making?' Felle thought with disdain, still piqued because Lia, when he had asked her, had closed the door in his face.

Then the other brothers arrived, bringing into the newly scrubbed and tidied kitchen the imprints of their snowy boots and the tang of the outdoors. They were all strong, good-looking men, with black eyes and black beards, their waistcoats as tight as breastplates beneath their lambswool tunics.

When the fiancé entered they all stood up, forming a semi-circle round their sister as if presenting a sort of bodyguard for that frail and delicate figure — not so much out of respect for the fiancé, who was still almost a boy, good-natured and timid, as for the man who accompanied him. This was the young man's grandfather. Over eighty years old but still upright and robust, dressed in garments of thick wool and velvet like a medieval nobleman, woollen leggings enveloping his sturdy limbs, this man, who had fought for Italy's independence, greeted the five brothers with a military salute and ran his eyes round the semi-circle as if inspecting them. And all of them seemed equally pleased with each other.

The old man was given the best seat, next to the fire, where the light playing on the shiny buttons of his tunic also illuminated, like a tiny star twinkling on his chest, his old medal for military valour. The bride-to-be poured him a drink, then poured one for her fiancé, who secretly slipped into her hand as he took the glass a gold coin.

She thanked him with her eyes, then covertly showed the money to her mother and all the brothers, in order of age, as she brought them their brimming glasses.

The last was Felle: and Felle tried to take the coin from her, as a joke and out of curiosity, of course; but she closed a menacing fist over it. She would rather have surrendered an eye.

The old man raised his glass in a toast of greetings and joy to all; and they all responded in chorus.

Then they began to discuss matters of common interest, but in an original way: by singing. The old man was an expert improviser of poems, that is, he could sing verses made up on the spot. And the eldest brother of the bride-to-be could do the same.

And so between the two of them there developed a kind of musical competition, on light-hearted topics of the day; and the others listened, joined in the choruses and applauded.

Outside, the bells were ringing, announcing Mass.

It was time to begin preparing dinner. The mother, helped by Felle, cut the legs off the two piglets and threaded them on to three long spits while he held the handles firmly against the floor.

'You can take a haunch to our neighbours as a present,' she told Felle. 'They have a right to enjoy the festival too.'

Very pleased, Felle took the fine plump leg of pork by the ankle and went out into the courtyard.

The night was frosty but calm, and suddenly it seemed as if the whole village had all sprung to life at once because, in the shimmering snowy whiteness and above the ringing of the bells, a clamour of shouts and songs seemed to be coming from everywhere.

In the neighbours' little house, however, everyone was silent. Even the little girls, who remained huddled round the stove, seemed to have fallen asleep, though still waiting, in their dreams, for some wonderful gift.

When Felle entered they shook themselves awake, looked at the leg of pork, which he was waving this way and that like a censer, but they did not speak: no, this was not the present they were waiting for. Meanwhile Lia had come running down from the little bedroom above. She took the present without ceremony, and to Felle's questions replied impatiently: 'Mama is feeling unwell; and papa has gone out to buy something special. Go away.'

He returned thoughtfully to his own house. There were no mysteries here, or sadness: all was life, movement and joy. Never had a Christmas been so merry, even when their father was still alive. Yet Felle nevertheless felt a little sad inside, thinking of the strange festivities in their neighbours' house.

When the bell for Mass rang for the third time, the fiancé's grandfather thumped his stick against the hearthstone.

'Right, you lads, up you get. Line up.'

And they all stood up to go to Mass. Only the mother remained at home, to look after the spits which were turning slowly before the fire and to see that the meat was thoroughly roasted.

So the sons, the betrothed couple and the grandfather, who seemed to be leading the company, made their way to church. The snow deadened their footsteps. Muffled-up figures emerged from all sides, lanterns in hand, throwing fantastical shapes of light and darkness all around. They exchanged greetings, they rapped on doors still closed to call everyone to Mass.

Felle walked as if in a dream. He did not feel the cold; on the contrary, the white trees surrounding the church seemed to him like almonds in flower. He felt, in fact, in his woollen clothes, as warm and as happy as a little lamb in the May sunshine. His hair, cooled by the snowy air, seemed to be made of springy grass. He was thinking of the good things he would eat when they returned from Mass, of his warmly heated house; and remembering that Jesus must instead be born in a cold stable, naked and hungry, there came over him a desire to cry, to cover him with his own clothes, to carry him back to his own house.

The illusion of spring continued inside the church: the altar was adorned with branches of arbutus with its red fruits, with myrtle and laurel. Candles shone among the fronds and their shadows rose along the walls as if on the walls of a garden.

In a side chapel stood the crib, with a mountain made from cork wood and covered with moss. The three Magi were coming cautiously down a steep hill, and a golden comet was lighting their way.

Everything was beautiful, all was light and joy. Powerful kings were leaving their thrones to bear their gifts of love and riches to the son of the poor, to Jesus born in a stable. The stars were their guide. The blood of Christ, who died for the happiness of mankind, fell in red drops on the bushes and made the roses bloom. It fell on the branches of the trees to

21

make the fruit ripen.

That was what the mother had taught Felle and that was how it was.

'Gloria, Gloria,' the priests sang from the altar. And the people responded: 'Glory to God in the highest of heaven.

'And peace on earth to men of good will.'

Felle was singing with everyone else, and he felt that this joy that filled his heart was the most beautiful present that Jesus was sending him.

Coming out of church he felt a little cold, because he had been kneeling all that time on the bare paving stones; but his joy was in no way diminished; rather, it grew stronger. At the smell of roasting meat coming from the nearest houses, he opened his nostrils, sniffing like a puppy, and he began to run to arrive in time to help his mama get everything ready for dinner. But everything was already done. His mother had spread a white linen tablecloth, on the floor, over a rush mat, and other mats round it. And, following the ancient practice, she had placed outside, under the lean-to shed in the courtyard, a plate of meat and a jug of mulled wine with strips of orange peel floating in it, because the spirit of her husband, if he were ever to return to this world, might be hungry.

Felle went to see: he set the plate and the jug higher up, on a plank in the open shed, so that wandering dogs could not reach them. Then he looked towards the neighbours' house as well, but all was silence. The father must not yet have returned with his mysterious gift.

Felle returned inside and took his full part in the feast that followed.

In the middle of the table rose a small tower of round and gleaming bread rolls looking as if they were made of ivory. Each of the guests from time to time leant forward and helped himself to one. The roast too, cut into thick slices, was set out on a number of wooden or earthenware platters, and everyone served themselves, as they pleased.

Felle, seated next to his mother, had pulled a whole plateful towards him, all for himself and was eating without paying heed to anything else. Obscured by the noise of his own teeth crunching the piglet's crisp skin, the chatter of the grown-ups seemed far away and held no interest any more.

When the tart was then brought to the table, yellow and warm as the sun, and surrounded by sweetmeats shaped like hearts, birds, fruits and flowers, he felt ready to faint away. He closed his eyes and leant on his mother's shoulder. She thought he might be crying: instead he was laughing with pleasure.

But when he was very full and felt the need to move about, he thought once more of his next door neighbours: whatever was happening to them? And had the father returned with the present?

An overwhelming curiosity drove him to go out into the courtyard again, creep up close and spy on them. The door, however, was ajar: in the kitchen the little girls were still gathered round the fire and the father, arriving late but in time nevertheless, was roasting on a spit the haunch of pork donated by his neighbours.

But the present bought by him, by the father, where was that?

'Come in, go upstairs and see,' the man told him, guessing

his thoughts.

Felle went in, climbed the wooden stairs, and in the little bedroom above, saw Lia's mother dozing in the wooden bed, and Lia kneeling before a wicker basket.

And inside, wrapped in warm linen cloths, lay a new-born baby, a fine pink baby with two curls of hair on its temples and its eyes already open.

'He's our first little brother,' Lia murmured. 'My father bought him at midnight exactly, while the bells were ringing the "Gloria". That means his bones will never fall apart, and he will find them all intact, on the Day of Judgement. That's the present that Jesus has given us tonight.'

IT'S STARTING TO SNOW

'Are we all inside?' my father asked, returning later than usual one evening, all muffled up and with his black silk scarf at his neck. And after a rapid glance around, he turned and bolted and barred the door as if a pack of thieves or wolves was bearing down on us. We little girls all jumped up and clustered round him, curious and fearful.

'What is it, what is it?'

'It's starting to snow, that's what it is. And it's going to carry on all night long and for a few days after that. The sky's the colour of a pigeon's breast.'

'Excellent,' said the little grandmother with satisfaction. 'Now you'll believe what I was telling you a moment ago.'

A moment ago the little grandmother, who in her brevity of stature and pinkness of complexion resembled us little girls, and who was more innocent and good than we were, was telling us for the thousandth time that one year, when she too really was a child (back in the first millennium, said the student brother, already a sceptic and with little respect for the sanctity of old age), a prolonged snowfall had buried and almost destroyed the village.

'Fourteen days and fourteen nights it snowed without stopping, without a minute's break. In the first few days, the young men and the bolder of the women too, went out into the streets on their horses and trampled the snow flat. And the servants made passageways through the middle of the white landscape the kitchen gardens and meadows had turned into. But then everyone shut themselves in their houses, not so much because of the snow as out of a feeling that some mysterious event was unfolding; a divine punishment. People began to believe the snow would last for all eternity and bury us all, inside our houses, which we were expecting to collapse at any moment. We had to do penance for our sins, all of us, even children who didn't respect their elders (I say that for you, master student); and all of us were scared we would die of hunger too.'

'You could have eaten the tender little children, as they did in the first millennium,' the impudent student boy insists.

'Enough. I feel sorry for you because you're at the ungrateful age,' says papa, who always finds a reason for excusing people. 'But with this kind of thing it's no joking matter. Just you see what a mountain of snow we'll have now. Listen to that, listen…'

There suddenly rose from the valley a great roaring of wind, filling the air with terror. And we children gathered round papa as if to hide under the tails of his coat.

'I've forgotten something. I need to go out for a moment,' he says, searching his pockets.

'I'll go, papa,' cries the boy, undaunted; but mama, white in the face, brings them all to a halt with a gesture.

'No, no, for goodness' sake, not now!'

'It's essential all the same,' papa insists, genuinely anxious. 'I forgot to buy any tobacco.'

Then mama's face clears and she goes to look for something in the cupboard.

'Tomorrow is St Anthony's; it's your feast-day, and I'd thought I'd give you a little present…'

She presents him with a pouch full of tobacco, and he bows his head, thanks her, says he treasures it as though it were full of gold. Meanwhile he allows his coat to be removed from his shoulders and sits at table to eat his dinner. Dinner is not as usual, animated and disturbed by incidents almost always provoked by the restlessness of the smallest of the diners: everyone is still and quiet, intent on the sounds from outside.

'But when the wind is this strong,' grandma says, 'it can't snow for long. That other time…'

And off she goes, telling it all again. And the terrible details of that other time increase our anxiety, which contains, however, just a touch of pleasure. It is like listening to a fable which at any moment could turn into reality.

What preoccupies us more than anything else is to know whether we have enough to survive on for the days of confinement that are coming.

'The hardest thing is milk: in this weather it's not easy to get any.'

But mama says she has a large tin of cocoa; and the news draws a snigger of joy from the boy, who hates milk. The other children do not dare copy him; but no one proclaims that the news is unwelcome. And also because it is known that besides the cocoa there exists a mysterious reserve of chocolate and, in case of extreme necessity, a jar of honey too.

There is no need for concern over the other necessities of life. There is wine and olive oil, cheese and flour, preserved meats and potatoes and other provisions, the cellar and the larder are overflowing. And there is no shortage of wood and coal. We were rich, then, and we didn't know it.

'And now,' says our father, rising from the table to take his seat beside the fire, 'I want to tell you the story of Giaffà.'

There then followed a real battle to secure the spot nearest to him; and even the voice of the wind grew still, to let us listen better. But grandma, alarmed by the silence outside, went to look out of the kitchen window, and said with uneasiness and pleasure: 'This time looks to me as if it's going to be just like that other time.'

All night it snowed, and the world, like a great ship letting in water, seemed to sink little by little into this white ocean. To us, it felt as though we were inside the great ship: we were going down, in our worst dreams, buried little by little, full of fear, yet buoyed by hope in God.

And the morning after, the good Lord made a brilliant winter sun spread its splendour over the pristine snow, in which the trunks of the poplar trees really did resemble the masts of a ship dressed overall in white.

PERHAPS IT WAS BETTER...

Alis was ten and had to go to school. Schoolwork, however, was not a thing he liked: he would have preferred to travel, or at least to be out in the street or in the fields, playing, especially with his puppy Bau, who would bounce and leap round him as if attached by a metal spring.

When he was actually forced to study, Alis developed headaches and prayed heaven for some momentous event to make schools and books disappear from the world.

And there came a night of wind and thunder when he heard his Bau whining and barking in the yard. Was it thieves? Alis was not frightened of thieves; on the contrary, he was curious to see some. He dressed therefore, as best he could, and went down to the yard. Instantly, by the light of the lamps, while the crashing of thunderclaps merged with a mysterious rumbling roar, he saw his house shake all over like a head saying yes and no, and then crack in pieces and collapse entirely. The other houses were falling down as well; and the church and the school too; and among the wreckage and other objects, text books could be seen tumbling over and over and exercise books flying about like great sinister butterflies.

It was an earthquake.

Seized with a wild terror, Alis began to run, followed by Bau. They ran, whipped along by the rain, the wind and the hail, as if the earthquake was pursuing them.

He ran and he ran until at last Alis saw, on the crest of a hill, a cottage with a light burning inside. When he got to the top he pushed at the door and found himself in a little room where a white-haired old woman was sleeping by the fire. A basket covered by a cloth was the only other object to be seen in the room.

Not wanting to wake the old woman, Alis huddled in a corner, with a trembling Bau pressed against him, and thanked God for having let him find this place of refuge.

The night passed, the storm quietened. Alis did not sleep, thinking of his collapsed house, which had become his family's tomb. So great was his grief that he was unable even to cry.

And as the sun rose, there appeared at the door a woman, barefoot and dressed all in green, and with a wand in her hand.

'Child,' she said, 'I know of your misfortune and I have come to collect you, if you wish to go with me. I am the Green Fairy: my home is here, beneath the earth, and if you come you will lack for nothing. You will live like a prince, I shall give you my daughter for your wife. But you must remain in my kingdom and never leave it.'

'And the dog?' Alis asked.

'The dog we cannot take because we fairies are afraid of dogs and cockerels. But he can stay here with this old woman, who is the Mother of the Winds and is about to wake up and prepare food for her sons, who are already on their way home. Well, do you wish to come?'

The puppy covertly tugged at the hem of his coat, as if to advise him to flee, not to go with the fairy. Alis was thinking. He was thinking that living all the time underground, even if it was the realm of the fairies, was not a very cheerful thing; on the other hand, where could he go? He had no home any more, no village, no relations, no friends.

'Do I have to go to school?' he asked.

'What school? The only thing you'll do is play.'

And he went.

The fairy led him to the foot of the hill and touched a stone with her wand; and at once they found themselves in a large and shining garden, standing before a palace all of marble.

'Where does the light come from if we are underground?' Alis wondered. And again he began to think.

The fairy did not seem disposed to offer him any explanations except what she could show him by waving her shiny, supple wand. With this she made the great doors of the palace open and close, with this she summoned the other fairies. They were all beautiful, the other fairies, whether big or little, but Alis noticed that, like birds and cats, like many other graceful creatures, they never smiled and neither did they ever do any work.

In any case, why should they work? Everything could be had at the mere touch of the wand. And what pleased Alis most of all was the complete absence in the palace of things that make men irritable: the telephone, electric lighting, stoves, doorbells, pianos, servants, objects with a scholastic purpose.

After showing him round the palace, the fairy led him to the dining room where the table was beautifully laid and spread with his favourite delicacies. And she introduced the young blonde fairy who was one day to be his wife.

This child, already quite tall, with eyes and dress the colour of a blue sky, delighted Alis as much as the sun, the moon and the other beautiful things of the earth. She too, however, never smiled, and when he suggested they go down into the garden to play, she stared at him in wonderment: she did not know what playing was.

'I'll teach you,' he told her under his breath. 'Let's go.'

They went down into the garden and he suggested and explained all the games he knew. She listened to him willingly, but she was unable to learn the games, or even to dance and to run. Then he began to grow bored and wished he had at least an adventure book to read.

And as evening came, his boredom turned to sadness. He thought about his ruined house, his dead relations. But were they all really dead in fact? Oh, why had he fled like a coward? Perhaps he could have lifted the fallen stones and saved someone. And also, his heart was gripped by remorse at having abandoned Bau, who after all had been his saviour. Perhaps it was better to stay in the cottage of the Mother of the Winds, wait for them to come back and then let himself be carried off by them.

Perhaps it was better... Yes, everything is better than doing nothing and simply getting, so easily, all the things one desires. Now he began to understand why fairies, even the young ones, cannot smile.

The grown-up Green Fairy perceived his sad thoughts at once.

'Listen to me,' she told him. 'I should give you the engagement ring for my daughter. In truth I wanted to offer you it later, in a few years' time, but perhaps it is better now.'

'Yes, perhaps it is better,' he replied dreamily.

Then the little girl, at a sign from her mother, slid a small silver ring over his finger; and suddenly he felt a different person. He forgot everything that had ever happened before, he felt light, without any thoughts, without any questions, without any curiosity, as happy as when one is ready to go to sleep.

He went down into the garden with the little girl and walked with her along the moonlit paths, stopping to look at the reflections in the lake, the play of the shadows and the strange colours of the roses.

And when he returned to his very attractive bedroom, he saw himself reflected in the mirrors like the moon in the lake: his eyes were soft and beautiful, but, like the eyes of deer, of cats, of turtle-doves, they no longer smiled.

THE LITTLE SILVER RING

In Sardinia there still exist fairy houses. Only these fairies were very small: as small as a two-year-old child, and not always good children, often bad ones. In dialect they were called *Janas* and there is still a curse in usage against anyone who might have done something to annoy us: '*Mala Jana ti jucat.*' May the bad fairy get you; in other words, come after you.

My dream as a little girl was to visit these fairy dwellings and go inside one. But with their being a long way from inhabited areas, for the most part distant and rocky places, the dream was not easy to achieve.

The highly-coloured stories that a farm worker used to tell whenever he came back to the village to change his shirt and go to Mass intensified my desire.

This young farmhand used to recount how he had visited

the houses of the *Janas* on many occasions, and would lower his voice as he described the details.

'The door is low and narrow, made from slabs of stone, and you have to go in on all fours. At first all you can see is a small room, a stone grotto where snakes and lizards hide away; but if you have the patience to search carefully, you will find a moveable stone that swings like a door, and this is the real entrance to the *Janas'* house. Again you need to crawl in on your hands and knees, but suddenly you find yourself in a room more than seven metres high, all gilded like a pulpit and with the ceiling painted with stars. And in front of you, you see hundreds of openings leading to a long line of rooms, each one more beautiful than the last, ending in a gallery overlooking the sea.'

This was the detail that fascinated the most: this opening out of the mysterious underground passage on to the vast panorama of the sea.

But little of what the farmhand said was credible. He was a young man given to seeing things, constantly ill with malarial fevers, who mistook what he saw in his delirium for the truth and was the first to believe it. In this way, he came to be familiar with a whole crowd of respectable characters, from the great devil to the imp '*Surtore*', who lives in people's houses but is never seen, and who hides things, provokes women to gossip, opens the door to the vampires who suck children's blood.

He recounted how he had seen, in the solitude of the mountains, a herd of deer guided by a herdsman who had antlers just like those of his agile flock, and this shepherd was the devil and the stags were the damned souls of thieves.

He recounted how he had seen on the seashore a beautiful small boy with golden hair and sky-blue eyes who was scooping up sea water in a shell and scattering it all around. And from the arid sand there sprang corn and vines; and this child was Jesus!

Giants and dwarves came and found him, when he was alone in the sheep-folds minding the sheep, especially on foggy days when it is easier to melt away and hide.

Last of all, he had in his possession a silver ring with a little pearl, which was a tiny piece of crystal in which the seven colours of the spectrum were reflected. Well, he insisted that one day, after a storm, he had managed to find the exact spot where the rainbow begins. He had dug down and discovered the ring, which allows whoever possesses it to invent a hundred and one stories in a single evening.

This little ring was the only concrete proof of all the things he claimed, because when it came to discovering tales of wonder, he could only do it when he was left on his own.

And this is what happened. In September one year, a September as mild and green as early spring, we found ourselves at Valverde, which is a very beautiful valley, all rocks and bushes, in whose lonely cleft sits a little church said to have been built long ago by a bandit as a penance, in expiation of his own sins.

A lovely spot, lovely days of sheer poetry: every hour a new line, every day a harmonious verse.

And then one Sunday our young farm labourer arrives, bringing a candle for the Lady of the little church on behalf of his disabled grandmother. After praying with great devotion and planting his candle, he came out and proposed to me and to a few of my friends that we go with him to see the houses of the *Janas*, which he said were only two steps from there.

And off he went. The two steps, however, seemed to double all by themselves, like the famous grains of millet in the legend: two, four, eight, sixteen, thirty-two, sixty-four, etcetera. Up we climbed, down we scrambled, along a rugged path: here we are, this is where the houses are, in that little rocky hill where certain menacing birds are cawing and flapping their wings with a sound like the whistling of the wind. To tell the truth, some of us are scared: what if those big black birds were wicked men transformed into their present shapes by the fairies?

The youth encourages us.

'Come along, can't you see they're just crows and ravens? There must be some carrion up there, a dead animal or a dead man and they're tucking in.'

One little girl falls to the ground and begins to cry.

'Serves you right,' he says, 'because you've come here without asking your parents' permission!'

And which of us has any such permission? We all ought to go tumbling back down to the bottom of the valley.

'Be brave, be brave, we're there: there's the door, can you see it? That one between those four rocks underneath a lentisk bush.'

Indeed, a black opening can be seen, but it is high up, among a pile of rocks, and only the birds can get at it.

And what if there was some man hidden up there, some bad man who wanted to do us harm? A sudden piercing whistle does in fact ring out, as if trying to drive us away; and the whole gang, including our bold guide, comes to a terrified halt.

To prove his courage to us, the boy advances and answers the whistle with a provocative whistle of his own, which seems to say: 'If you've got any guts, come out.'

The whistle is not repeated, but from high up among the rocks there begins to come down a hail of stones which hit some of the company. The menacing birds cry: 'Serves you right, serves you right, little girls: going off in search of adventures without your parents' permission.'

The boy begins to yell, his hands cupped round his mouth, insulting the hidden enemy and calling him to come out. Then he shouts:

'Stand back, everyone,' and launches an assault up the rocky hillside.

But just as he arrives at the opening which according to him was the fairies' door, a treacherous hand dislodges him and he tumbles back, rolling like a ball of wool, fortunately without doing himself any great damage, leaving shreds of clothing caught on the bushes and losing all the things in his pocket.

Two heads of horrible small boys then appear in the opening, guffawing; and even we ungrateful creatures below laugh at our poor guide. We laugh and run away; even the young man is compelled to beat a retreat because another terrible volley of stones comes hurtling down; and in his revenge-threatening indignation he does not notice that he has lost the little silver ring. And it was I instead who picked up the ring, and I have it still.

THE HOUSE OF THE MOON

The same boy who led us with such minimal results on the search for the house of the fairies, claimed that he knew where the house of the moon's mother was, and also the dwelling of the mother of the winds.

This one is harder to find, because it stands on top of the mountains. They winds play in front of it, like boys in the yard, and are capable of knocking you to the ground with their breath, or of hurling you against boulders and tree trunks. The house of the mother of the moon is more easily accessible for anyone with a little natural pluck and courage. All one needs to do is take careful note of the precise point where the moon rises in the evening for its beautiful passage through the blue meadows of the sky; there, the mother lives.

'And the father, where is he?'

'The father is the sun, and everyone knows where he is,

but it would be pointless to think of going to look for him.'

Anyway, why this urgent desire to know the moon's mother? She will be a little old woman dressed in pearly white who prepares bed and food for her restless daughter. But the wish to know her is not for her own sake; it is for her house hidden behind the trees lining the crest of the hill or maybe beyond the vineyard: a house made all of silver, with balconies of gold and diamonds for doornails.

The moon rose behind the vines, in those still warm October evenings, evenings seemingly intoxicated by the smell of the first pressing and by that of the still unharvested strawberry grape.

The vineyard was enormous, undulating across a single uncultivated plain. Tall fig-trees threw their heavy shadows on the green of the vines, and their fruit dropped to the ground by themselves, slowly, like fat drops of concentrated honey. Who ate figs in those days? They were regarded with disgust and flicked out from under one's feet with the point of a stick. The grapes did not please us any better, not even the muscatel variety with fruit the size of plums; we preferred the last blackberries gleaming on the bushes in the fields beyond the vineyard.

A small cottage, which could barely have had two rooms, appeared before us out of the misty night; overhead, a pine tree murmured, even though there was no wind to stir it; and its soundless music seemed to open wide the roof of the building, a mere cabin, and bear us away in slow spiralling circles, in a silken network, far away through the infinite space of dreams.

Among these dreams, then, there began to predominate the dream of going in search of the house of the moon.

Besides, what could be difficult about it? One had only to climb the path through the vines again, jump over the low boundary wall, an act of bravery accomplished more than once, go as far as the briar bushes, taking care not to prick oneself, and reach the crest of a short grassy slope. That is where the ever rounder moon shows its face on those bountiful October evenings, a face round and placid like someone who has been indulging in the fruits of the vine.

And one evening the idea is put to the test. There is a night-time celebration in the vineyard. A farmhand is playing the accordion and the girls are dancing in the light of the moon. So there is no danger of encountering the wolf, who doesn't like music and stays away until the noise has stopped. I go. I have to say in confidence that I do not really believe the house of the moon exists. But I am going to look for it out of a spirit of adventure and rebellion more than anything else, and to prove my courage.

And the moon looked down on me askance, with a wry face which reminded me of one of my companions in the garden games of my infancy. I still retain the memory of walking through the vineyard with the impression that all the low grey vine plants, under the moon, were so many sleeping sheep. The sound of the accordion gave me company.

The wall is duly jumped over, and here the world changes its aspect: it is still a known world, with its stones and bramble bushes, but it is no longer ours. A trace of nervousness sets in: who moved and made the grass glitter at my feet? No need to be frightened; it is probably a lizard; at any event, I need to stay alert.

The music sounds rather distant, but it doesn't stop. It is

43

like the voice of an accomplice who has stayed behind to make sure the escapade is not discovered.

Here is the short grassy incline behind which the famous dwelling should be located. Why I take off my shoes and socks I still don't know. Perhaps to approach in greater silence, or because I was absolutely forbidden to do such a thing. What I do know is that a large thorn immediately informed me, by driving itself into my right heel, that I had done wrong.

I sat on the grass and tried, by the light of the moon, to pull the thorn out: impossible. It went even further in and I thought it would work its way right up to my heart.

I put my socks and shoes back on, but remained there, on the thin-bladed grass, seized by an inexplicable terror. Now I shall get gangrene, they will amputate my foot, and that way God will punish me for wanting to go walking at night outside the bounds of my own property, for disobeying my parents.

To increase my discomfort, now the music suddenly stops. I seem to be alone in the world, or worse still in the middle of a pack of wolves, advancing, silent and terrible, swishing their long yellow tails on the ground.

Then I heard my name being called, far away, and I desperately retraced my steps until I was once more climbing over the wall. And I said nothing about the thorn, which would not come out however much I poked at it with a needle. As long as the foot did not swell up and begin to suppurate, I kept quiet and waited every day for the terrible punishment. Nevertheless, sitting by the window of the little bedroom, with my bare foot wrapped up, I looked towards the crest of the hill where the moon was born, a little later in the evening every day. On the third day the foot became swollen. And in the evening the moon did not appear, but instead, on the crest of the hill, a fantastical castle, made of tissue paper, with decorations of gold and silver. It was a cloud, but, to my joyous heart, this looked like the true house of the moon.

BREAD

Until I was nearly a grown woman, it was my job at home to make the bread. That was what my mother wanted, and that was what had to be done. Not for reasons of economy, since we were at that time, by the grace of God, well off, better off than we thought, but because it was a domestic tradition. And domestic traditions, in our house, were religion and law.

Harsh law: having to get up before dawn, when a young person's slumber holds her in its velvet clasp and has absolutely no desire to let her go!

The daily help knocks at the door, lamp in hand, she too wavering slightly from her interrupted sleep. Up, up, it's time to get up. One foot pokes out from under the eiderdown but promptly withdraws, as if it has been dipped in cold water, while the other foot is still in the warm land of dreams. An arm

47

stretches out and the hand clenches nervously while the other remains blissfully spread on the soft sheet, as if on a field of daisies in the sun. The daily help knocks a second time, then pushes on the door.

'Up, up, or the mistress will come down…'

Then the foot that is awake prods the one that is still asleep and the hand that is awake searches out the hand that is dreaming… And the pair of them draw on all their courage. We are standing up. How cold it is! How hard life is! But one of these days…

Well, yes, I must confess that by the time I was twelve I had firmly resolved to get married so as not to have to make bread at home any more.

But once these first moments had passed, the business took on a rhythm of its own, almost a ritual.

It needs to be said that this business was not a daily thing, or even weekly, because the double-baked loaves which we typically but appropriately called 'music cases' lasted entire months without spoiling, especially in winter.

Especially in winter it was good, in the big kitchen heated by the fires lighted in both stove and hearth: outside there was snow. Worse off than us was the little woman who had chosen the trade of 'bread-minder'. No, this person did not allow herself to be seduced by her slumbers, and every day, and often every night as well, she spent her time standing in front of the bread oven, battling with those large round focaccia loaves which have a tendency to swell, to burst and to burn in a flash, and it appears they do it out of spite against the paddle that flips them over and flips them back again and smacks them like a mother's hand on the plump buttocks of naughty children.

This woman, then, also had to brave the cold and the snow to arrive at her destination. Once there, however — this is in winter, you understand — she was the happiest person in the world. She would sit in front of the oven and be served like a queen; and a queen from a puppet show is what she looked like: small, her limbs like sticks, her face toasted black from the ovens of all the village and with a voice which seemed to come from far away, from the very top of the oven's stove-pipe. The things she would tell us were all interesting, especially after she had taken coffee or eaten three plates of macaroni and drunk a good glass of wine.

This wine, to tell the truth, was given to her by me. Secretly, because at that time it was not the custom for women to drink wine (though privately they did). She would turn to the wall pretending very realistically to blow her nose, and would drink with her head bent, greedily sucking from the glass. Or else I gave it to her in a tin cup as if it were water poured from the pitcher.

My mother, who always spoke in hushed tones as if praying, because when bread is being made it is like being in church, did not notice the bread-minder's sin.

The bread-minder would become loquacious and could relate the history of every family in town, including those of their ancestors. And my imagination went trawling in these recitals more than it did in printed volumes of adventures and facts.

When I had finished kneading the dough and rolling out

the loaves with a rolling pin, and with the pearls of blisters that the operation left on the smooth palms of my hands, I would sit next to the woman and listen.

To relate all her stories would be to write ten more books, apart from those safely committed to paper already. For today, I shall recall just one, which must have been true, since the woman often told it, and with never a single variation, whereas the others frequently underwent several modifications.

'So,' these are her exact words, ' - it's many years ago now, almost as soon as the Lord had given me the strength to work and my mother had given me the knowledge - there I am one day, going to see to the bread in *donna* Barbara's house. *Donna* Barbara was very rich and miserly, so much so that they say she died with her fists clenched, whereas good Christians relax their hands as they consign their souls to God. *Donna* Barbara gave me a handful of dried figs in the morning, she didn't even give me a bit of fresh bread. Even dogs get a bit of fresh bread, on baking day. Dry bread and as much water as I wanted. In fact she encouraged me to drink because drinking water stops you from wanting to eat. But now I'm going to tell you how God sent me satisfaction a hundred times over. One morning at dawn, then, when the cocks were crowing, and while we were waiting for the bread to rise the proper amount, lo and behold a boy comes to the door, a beautiful child with curly fair hair and sky-blue eyes. His little red smock was faded and torn — and yet it looked brand new.

'"Give me a scrap of bread," he says, "even if it's as small as a consecrated wafer. It's such a long time since I ate fresh-made bread."

'"Straightaway, pretty child," says *donna* Barbara, who

was truly a gentlewoman as far as good words go. "And who are you? Why are you up and about so early?"

'The child doesn't answer, and the lady, taking the scraps of dough left on the table, rolls them into a tiny loaf and gives it to me to cook.

'I put the little loaf in the oven, and see an extraordinary thing.

'The loaf grows and it grows, it grows until it fills the whole floor of the oven: I have to fold it in four to get it out. Do you think *donna* Barbara gives it to the child? Not a crumb. She takes all the remains of the left-over dough and makes a miniature loaf the size of a penny. Well, this one also grows and it grows. And she, by now mad with joy, begs the child to wait and meanwhile continues to make tiny little loaves of dough and give them to me; and I'm sweating to get them out, so big have they turned in the oven — until the Lord shines on me the light of understanding, and I say, straightening up and kneeling: "*Donna* Barbara, this child is Jesus in person, come to test the goodness of our hearts." *Donna* Barbara turns round: the child has vanished. And when she tastes one of those enormous loaves she has to spit it out because it's so sour. And in the baskets where the dough has been left to rise, all the rest of the bread has also gone bad. Thus was *donna* Barbara punished for her sour heart.'

THE BASKET OF GRAPES

Primo, Secondo and Terzo, the three Gelmini brothers, had set out to take a basket of grapes to their grandmother. Not that their grandmother didn't have any grapes of her own: on the contrary, she had so many that her trellis was more black than green. But as for quality, only the Gelmini family, in all the district, had such fine grapes, and possibly no finer grapes were known anywhere in the world. So much so that their mother warned the three boys to keep the basket well covered with the cloth, and if anyone asked what was in the basket, they were to reply: 'It's eggs and peppers.'

'It's eggs and peppers,' the three brave brothers did indeed reply in chorus when Vica the hunchback, the woman who lived on the streets, and who trotted along behind passers-by like a dog without a master to avoid being mistreated, jumped down from the bushes marking the boundary of someone's small-holding and asked what was in the basket.

'That's not true,' she said, fixing her little yellow eyes on the flimsy cloth that failed to disguise the outlines of the bulging bunches. 'What you've got there are grapes, the sort that only grow on the trellis behind your house. I know all about it: the fruits are long and pointed like spicy peppers, but the taste is different from anything else. I've never tried it for myself though. Will you let me have a taste?'

'Get away from here!' Primo shouted, brandishing a menacing fist. And the other two brothers gathered closely round the basket, defending it like the sacred ark of the Hebrews in the desert.

The spot was indeed deserted, and the houses of the grandmother's hamlet were not yet in sight. If she had wanted, the hunchback, who may have had a hunched back but was very solid, could have routed the three intrepid brothers with her stick: but she did not want to. She already enjoyed enough fame as a malicious woman, a thief, an importuner and bringer of misfortune; so she contented herself with humiliating and frightening the Gelminis.

'I thought you were better than this! You are ill-mannered and mean. And the Madonna will punish you for having refused three grapes to a poor beggar woman with no home and no bread.'

The youngest of the Gelmini then seemed about to give the hunchback a small bunch of grapes — out of fear, that is, not out of love — but the other two, and especially Primo, who already had the hard heart of an old peasant, vehemently opposed him.

And all three walked on, while Vica disappeared among

the bushes from which she had emerged. To while away the long stretch of road ahead of them, Primo suggested a game.

'You two are the oxen pulling the cart. The cart's full of grapes and I'm the driver.'

'We'll take turns: I don't want to be an ox all the time, I don't,' Secondo said.

The proposal accepted, the two younger brothers took the basket between them and advanced. Primo urged them on, and discontented with their efforts armed himself with a leafy switch and began to flick it at their legs. Secondo started to run, but the smallest brother, who was already tired and cross, let go of the basket handle, and a large portion of the grapes spilled out on the ground. The beautiful bunches disintegrated like so many necklaces whose threads have broken.

The yells of Primo and the blows he rained on his little brother did nothing to repair the damage. Nor did the observation Secondo made: 'It's because the hunchback brings bad luck. And we refused to give her even one small bunch of grapes.'

That was the first of their misfortunes.

The second came about when they decided to leave the road and take a footpath across the fields, which would bring them to the grandmother's house sooner. Little Terzo, who since his vigorous treatment at the hands of his big brother had not stopped snivelling and complaining, stumbled awkwardly in a hole in the path concealed by the grass, and fell full length, banging his face on the ground. At first he did not cry out, he did not attempt to get up; but when his brothers, alarmed by his silence, pulled him to his feet, he began to bite them and aim kicks at them.

He had blood on his face and seemed to have gone insane.

'What's got into you?' Primo shouted, pushing him over on the grass again. There they held him down by force and wiped his face with the cloth from the basket. He was weeping so hard that his tears helped clean his face. Then he refused to follow his brothers. But when they walked on and disappeared behind a stretch of millet growing as tall and thick as a forest and he found himself alone, he became frightened. On both sides of the footpath the statuesque ranks of maize looked to his eyes like soldiers with their bayonets fixed, and a strange rustling, produced by the waving of the hard leaves, reminded him that wolves like to roam in fields where the vegetation is thick. He had never seen a wolf, but he imagined it as being big and fierce like the wolf depicted in the painting of Saint Francis in his mama's bedroom — and that it made no distinction between chickens and small boys.

He thought then that it would be a good idea to get up and hurry after his brothers, to regain the safety of their company; but however much he hurried, he could not catch them up. Not only that, he couldn't even see them in the distance. Then he really began to be frightened. He believed he was lost, and was about to shout for help (from whom, if there was not a living soul in sight?) when a flapping of goose wings brought him a little reassurance. If there were geese about, there were probably Christians as well, because no one has ever heard of geese living in the desert. These ones, on the contrary, were making that special honking they reserve for when someone comes along; and they redoubled their noise on seeing little Terzo. They seemed very cheerful, all gathered together in a group of nine or ten, looking like a flock, all white and with small and round black eyes like shoe buttons.

Terzo, however, did not share their pleasure; in fact he went pale in the face as if about to faint, and gave a shout of horror. Because in their midst he saw the basket of grapes, empty. The geese had pulled out, stripped and destroyed every bunch, not leaving a single one.

What had happened to the other brothers? The wolves, clearly, had leapt on them and devoured them and nothing remained of them, not even the laces from their shoes. Stupid with grief, Terzo retrieved the cloth which had covered the basket and with it, stained as it already was with his own blood, he wiped his tears, tears that were as big as the fruit of the grapes still scattered on the ground.

'It's the hunchback, it's the hunchback...' he sobbed. He meant: it was the hunchback who brought this misfortune on us, but he could not finish the sentence because his thoughts were so confused. Nevertheless he picked up the basket as well and set off to return the way he had come.

The yells of Primo called him back.

'What are you doing, you monkey? Hey, what are you doing?'

He turned round, and saw his two brothers, safe and sound, each with a quince in his hand. Secondo, in fact, had two, one of them half eaten. And this explained his silence and his wry face, because the fruit was so bitter and hard that it stuck in his throat and he couldn't speak.

From the shouting and abuse of Primo, Terzo then understood how this affair had come about. The older brother knew there was a quince tree in the field, and wanting to steal its fruit, had ordered Secondo to wait for him on the footpath with the basket of grapes. But Secondo had no intention of obeying. He had planted the basket on the ground so that he too could go and pick the quinces. What Terzo could not succeed in understanding was why the brothers took it out on him. Primo, the eldest, then the other one, started shoving him again and punching him, accompanying him like that all the way to their grandmother's house.

'It's your fault. It's all your fault.'

Terzo no longer defended himself, no longer wept, no longer understood anything at all; but when they arrived at the grandmother's and the brothers told the story, after their own fashion, he asked: 'Why, if I was the one who wanted to give the hunchback some grapes, then why has all the bad luck happened to me? Why?'

'Because you are the smallest and the stupidest,' the grandmother explained, blowing his nose for him.

THE VOW

That long-ago winter was an ill-omened one for my small town of Nuoro. Even though I was a child, I remember it as I don't remember recent times. To begin with, it snowed for fourteen days in succession; then torrential rains fell, making walls collapse; finally diphtheria, then called angina, played havoc among the children.

The only son of our tenant farmer, Chischeddeddu Palasdeprata, was also afflicted. The father was a man of probity and an indefatigable worker; the nickname Palasdeprata — silverback — had stuck to him for that reason; the mother, in that case, was a woman of gold: wise, strong, devout.

When she saw her son dying she knelt on her doorstep, facing the vast landscape of the Orune and Lula mountains, and prayed aloud: 'Saint Francis, my beloved saint, you who stand calmly in your church up there in the hills, listen to me.

Make my Francesco, my little white lamb, better and I will come to your church shoeless, on my bare feet, in pilgrimage, and I will bring you as a gift all the money that I and my husband have received from a whole year of our work.'

The child suddenly felt better, and a week later he was cured.

Now came the matter of fulfilling the vow. Chischeddeddu was seven and went to school but he intended to work on the land like his father; as a result his head was filled with no flights of fancy, and when he returned from school he took off his shoes and threw them aside as if they were encumbrances.

He was, however, like all Sardinian children, a bit of a dreamer; when the time approached for the vow to be fulfilled he began to act restlessly, saying that Saint Francis had appeared to him in the street and invited him to accompany his mother on her pilgrimage.

And so the two of them set off, one morning at dawn in the beautiful month of May when the days are rich in golden hues and perfumes. The woman carried on her head a little basket containing her shoes and her son's, and a little bread and hard cheese; and tucked away in her bosom she had the money, tightly wrapped in a red headscarf. The path was difficult, for it involved the constant climbing and descending of steep gradients; in return, though, the places they passed through were very lovely: tall grasses, flowers, green bushes and thickets. From time to time a little spring of crystal clear water emerged as if by miracle from among the moss-covered stones, and then there came from the stands of uncultivated trees the song of the nightingale, who seemed to be thanking

God for the incomparable gift of this water. Mother and son halted beside one of the springs to rest and eat. The woman leaned over the shallow basin where the water gleamed like the sun, and before she drank she dipped a hand in it and crossed herself. Chischeddeddu instead washed his burning feet and said he wanted to climb a steep rock towards an oak tree full of nightingales' songs to see if he could find a nest.

'We'll put them in the basket and take them home.'

But the mother forbade it, for even if she was not an educated woman, she knew that Saint Francis dearly loved all birds.

To console himself, the boy began to throw stones, frightening the nightingales, and then to shout loudly to hear his voice echoing in the hills.

Suddenly, as if disturbed and irritated by the unaccustomed racket in this deserted spot, a man appeared in an opening in the scrub. He was dressed entirely in black, his beard was black too, and in his dark face his eyes shone like the water in the pool.

He carried no gun, but the woman guessed straightaway that they had stumbled on a bandit hiding in the hills to escape the searching *carabinieri*. But she did not panic. She simply turned her eyes towards the sanctuary of Saint Francis, which could already be seen like a white fortification up in the mountains amid the flowering broom; and she seemed to hear a voice telling her: 'Have no fear.'

The man in black picked his way down the precipitous track with great agility, and the nightingales fell silent as he passed. So did the boy, clinging tightly and wordlessly to his mother — although gratified, deep down, to see a bandit up close and thus to be able to describe him, if in slightly exaggerated terms, to his companions and friends. But curiosity turned to shivers of anxiety when he noticed this fearsome man, coming closer and casting an eagle-eyed glance all round to check they were completely alone, fix his gaze not so much on the mother as on the boy himself. And his memories from early childhood, with the old Ogre who lives in the woods and carries children off to his lair to fatten them up and eat them over a roasting spit, half raw and half cooked, did little to boost his courage. Even his mother, now, could feel her heart beating, as if she and her little Francesco were the fledgling nightingales in the nest, plucked from the oak tree and put in the basket by a cruel hand.

'What are you doing here?' the man said, as angrily as if he owned this place absolutely and these two miserable wretches were invading his property.

The woman recounted the story of the vow. She said nothing, however, of the money concealed on her person.

The man was still looking at the boy and seemed to address himself to him alone.

'Ah, you're the son of Palasdeprata? Yes, I've heard of him, yes! It seems he's got an earthenware crock full of gold pieces hidden under a tree, your father — I'd like to make him dance with a bullet or two under his feet — that's what I hear. Well, we'll make him dig it up. Money ought to circulate. You'll stay with me, little billy-goat, and your mother will go and get the pot. She will bring it here, leave it here, and she'll go away again. Then I'll set you free, in the little place I'll take you to once your mother's gone. At any rate, you know the way. That's if you don't prefer to stay with me. Oh, there's

62

no need to wail, woman. Up on your feet and start walking.'

The mother was crying, clinging to her boy, and through the veil of her tears the white church of Saint Francis looked as if it was decorated with diamonds: no, the Saint couldn't, mustn't abandon her.

'My husband does not own a penny,' she said. 'Everything we have is here. Take it, but let us go.'

She appeared to rip the very heart from her breast and throw it at the man's feet. It was the little red scarf with the money inside. But the man didn't even deign to look at it.

'On your feet, and go,' he repeated.

Then mother and son, clutching each other in desperation, began to weep noisily; and she called out: 'My Saint Francis, help me.'

The echo answered, and it seemed like the voice of the Saint.

Another man appeared in the same opening the first had emerged from, but the first man showed no alarm; in fact he seemed to be expecting him, in the way one might await reinforcements; for he too was a man who lived up here in the hills.

How different, though! He was an old man with a white beard and blue eyes, his face furrowed with deep creases which appeared to have been carved over the course of some long grief. Dressed in the old style, with a hemp smock tied about the waist with a rope, he seemed to the woman to be a hermit sent by Saint Francis to help her. He came calmly down the steep track, tapping with his stick the green trunks of the trees as if to reassure himself that no one was hiding in the hollows, and when he stopped beside his companion he

63

too looked particularly at Chischeddeddu. But it was a look of nostalgia, as if he had not set eyes on a boy for years beyond number, and this one reminded him of his own childhood and the little brothers and companions of his innocence. Then, while the bandit explained why they were all here together, he turned to the woman: 'My dear, charming creature, you did wrong to set out on a journey like this, through places you knew were inhabited by the devil.'

Already reassured, the woman smiled at him; and even Chischeddeddu clamped his tongue, still salty with tears, between his teeth, so that the man in black should not see, and also to prevent himself from bursting out laughing. The mother replied to the old man, partly convinced already, partly to flatter and pacify him further: 'You are not a devil, you are a saint, and that is why Saint Francis has sent you.'

On hearing the name of the Saint, the old man removed his cap and crossed himself. Then he said: 'Go, woman: and we will escort you on the rest of the journey ourselves, to make sure nothing bad happens to you or to this kid-goat, your son. However, when you get to the Sanctuary, you will say a Hail Mary for me.'

Then the bandit hung his head in mortification and murmured: 'And for me too.'

And picking up the little red scarf, which blazed against the grass like a flower, he placed it back in the woman's hands.

MIRELLA

At times we doubt the existence of God. Because, in the end, where is this God? In heaven on earth in all things: yes, fine. But the fact is, no one has ever seen him.

So God, to prove to us his existence, ordains the arrival of a beautiful day.

Not a spring day, or summer, or autumn, but a winter day.

It is the most beautiful of all; it is the sapphire in the ring that joins the years.

All the windows open to the sun, all the senses to joy.

And then one really does feel the presence of God in heaven on earth and in all things.

To make things perfect, Mirella comes among us.

This Mirella is five years old, and even though she doesn't yet know how to read, she carries under her arm the 'Children's

Daily News'.

She is all pink and fresh like coral newly brought out of the sea.

Her pretty little coat is soft and red, her cap is red. It is the cap worn by little girls on Sardinia, decorated with antique embroidery. And Mirella's black eyes with their golden flecks are also those of the children of Sardinia: they are the bewitching eyes that appear in the old stories and whose gaze is reputed to have an almost divine power.

But the way Mirella expresses herself, her way of speaking and especially her way of observing things, are fundamentally Tuscan. And the reason for this is that Mirella's papa once made a journey from the mountains of Pistoia to the mountains of Nuoro in search of a wife together with whom to make Mirella.

While we are out in the garden enjoying the sun, a man who is a scholar drops in for a moment.

Hardly has his keen eye fallen on Mirella than he says: 'That one will be a great woman!'

He does not explain why; in any event, when he has gone, it occurs to us to interview the future great woman.

'What are you going to do, Mirella, when you grow up?' we ask her, not without a certain sense of anxiety.

And our hearts expand, because Mirella answers: 'I want to go and dance.'

And she says it a little impatiently and emphatically, in a tone which means: how can you possibly not know that?

'I also want to be a gardener,' she adds after a moment's thought.

'And why is that?'

'Because there are cherries and grapes in your garden, and trees to climb on.'

And certainly she has so far shown a strong propensity for climbing things. Her feet, like a bird's, seem unable to stay long on the bare earth.

Mirella nevertheless has a great aptitude for working in the garden.

She excavates and handles the soil with pleasure, lifts heavy buckets of water, discovers insects still unknown to the rest of us. And she is not afraid of worms, which she dangles on the end of a twig to try to scare us, laughing at her own roguishness.

And she knows how to hoe even before she knows how to write.

Our conversations are not always frivolous, as for example when playing the game of *signora* Maddalena's visit, and this *signora* Maddalena, who is Mirella, talks of clothes and, little gossip that she is, criticises her friends and makes fun of them. No, at times our conversations reach worrying levels.

Here is Mirella, for example, squeezing herself beside me and whispering in my ear: 'God is surrounded by wolves.'

'Wolves? What for?'

'I don't know. He's got wolves all round him.'

'God has angels all round him,' I say, somewhat alarmed. 'Who thought it was a good idea to tell you such a horrid thing, that God is surrounded by wolves?'

'Allina told me.'

'Go and call Allina at once.'

Allina can be called by simply walking to the end of the garden. Mirella, however, seizes the opportunity to climb on top of the big gate and from there into the denuded lime tree, and from up there her voice carries like the sharp scent of the lime flowers in May.

'Allina! Allina! Allina, come here!'

A few moments later Allina is with us.

'Now, what's this story? Why did you say God is surrounded by a host of wolves? Are those the kind of things to tell a child?'

'But I didn't say anything of the sort.'

'Mirella! Why this lie? Who was it who told you…'

'Oh,' she interrupts, 'I made it up for myself.'

What will become of Mirella?

We don't think about it: for now it is better to let her dash after her bowling hoop, or throw stones at the other children, or try out, singing to herself, the first steps and the flattering poses of the ballet.

> Mirella goes dancing, her fingers be-ringed,
> A hundred on that hand, a hundred on this;
> One day a husband, one day a first kiss,
> Mirella goes dancing, her feet are be-winged.

THE SHEPHERD LAD

Five years or so ago I knew a young lad nicknamed Coeddu
— Pig's tail — a name also given to the devil, who, as you
know, is often represented with a little curly tail at the base of
his spine. Coeddu did indeed have the colouring of the little
rascal, although his features bore the signs of every breed of
humanity: he had the snub nose of an Ethiopian, the slanting
eyes of a Japanese, the thin and sarcastic mouth of a North
American, and the intelligent expression of a young Sardinian
lad, the authentic Nuoro look. He lived not far from our house,
and we often gave him some minor errand to do. He would
fly off to accomplish it, but once his task was done, he sat on
the ground and would remain for hour after hour immobile,
listless. If anyone stopped and questioned him, however, he
would start chattering away and never stop. One morning I
found him sitting under the ilex in our kitchen garden, sitting

cross-legged, motionless as an Arab boy in the shade of a palm. His enormous bare feet bore the punctures of dozens of thorns and tiny shards of glass. His curly hair was covered in dust and bits of straw.

'Do you go to school?' I asked him.

'Yes,' he answered, raising his sly eyes at me. 'I'm first in the class; I'm to go up into the third year and I'll be top there too.'

'Bravo! It must mean you like studying.'

'No, I like being a shepherd, because shepherds sleep during the day, when it's hot, and keep watch at night, when it's cool.'

'Ah, but what about in winter?'

'In winter they light a big fire, roast a whole sheep and eat it!'

'And what about now, what do you eat now?'

'Barley bread.'

'Always?'

'Always barley bread.'

'Doesn't your mother cook?'

'My mother works in service and only gets home at night.'

'And your father?'

'My father ran away. He went to America and erected us.'

He meant to say "rejected", but just then, in the mouth of that robust and intelligent boy planted on the ground like a little tree newly dug in, the word was appropriate.

'Your father will write to you, sometimes, though. And you'll write back.'

'Me?' he said fiercely. 'Never! I don't need him. I'm going to be a shepherd, and I'm going to find a treasure among the rocks, yes, one of those treasures hidden by giants and guarded by the devil. Yes, I know the places, because I often go up the mountain to gather bundles of wood, which I take to the mill. Two lire's worth of wood I can carry, all in one go. I'm strong: I only have to shake a tree and it falls over. I catch hawks in flight. I can imitate crows, wolves, all the animals. Do you want to see? One day I hit a rock with the axe and I heard a noise like money. Jingle, jangle, jingle, jangle. It's a sign there's treasure there. My uncle Mauro, who's a shepherd, knows where this treasure is too, but I won't tell anyone the exact spot he named. No, I won't tell; I'm not a spy, not me…

'Spies,' he continued, 'always get punished. When you know a secret you have to keep quiet about it. The other boys I go about with don't know how to keep a secret, and if they see someone do something wrong they go and tell on him straightaway. Not me. Not a spy and not a thief. Have you ever caught me stealing apricots and figs from your orchard at Concia?'

'Who knows, who knows…?'

'No, never, I swear!' he shouted, crossing his arms over his chest in confirmation of his oath. 'It's the other boys, they're the thieves. What'll you give me to tell you their names?'

'How can you do that if you're not a spy?'

He stared at me, unperturbed, but did not answer.

The same day I happened to meet his mother, a poor woman, thin and yellow, and asked her how her son was behaving.

'Don't talk to me about it, *sennòra* Grassia. He's not a bad boy, but he's so mischievous that the master, in despair, wanted to give him a lira to stay away from school. I send him out to gather firewood and instead he throws the rope over a branch and makes a swing. I've written to his father to bring him over to stay with him in America and at least teach him to work.'

When he discovered his mother was thinking of sending him to America, Coeddu became even more uncontrollable and mistrustful. He didn't want to know anything about the thing called civilisation. He didn't want to travel: he was content with his explorations on Mount Orthobene, where he always hoped to find treasure. One day in early August, his mother showed him a letter and told him: 'Take care, my boy, your father's written from America and agrees to have you with him. As soon as he's got the money for the journey he's going to send it to me.'

Coeddu started to cry, threw himself on the floor and shouted: 'Yes, tell him to send it, that money of his: I'll buy sheep with it and become a shepherd. I will work, yes, I will. Give me the rope, from today I'll take a bundle of wood to the mill every day…'

The mother, softening, gave him the rope and a piece of black bread, but he wanted white bread, and since there was none in the house, the poor woman had to go to a neighbour and borrow some.

And the boy set off, determined to do everything he had said, just to avoid going to America. But on the way he met two beggar boys who went up Mount Orthobene each morning to beg for alms among the summer visitors who came to camp every year round the little church of the Madonna of the Mountains for the festival; and he heard one of them say: 'Today for sure we'll be eating macaroni with chicken gravy.'

The other licked his grimy lips and smacked his tongue on the roof of his mouth.

'Today for sure we'll be eating pears, those yellow ones, floury as potatoes…'

At first Coeddu laughed at them; then he asked thoughtfully: 'Who gives you these nice things?'

'The serving women, up there. We bring them the firewood and get all these nice things in exchange.'

The path was steep and dusty; but when they reached the top, the three boys could see the sea, glistening like gold, with a little range of blue hills before it, and felt as cool as if the seashore were just nearby. Around the little church a village of tents and small huts had sprung up. Girls dressed in yellow and blue scampered through the woods, tiny creatures beneath the age-old oaks and enormous outcrops of rock, like multi-coloured butterflies.

Coeddu was mistaken for a beggar too: a brown-haired serving-woman, with a tanned face and honey-coloured eyes, as beautiful as a Samaritan, gave him the job of collecting some firewood from the forest to cook the macaroni; and then she gave him a portion. He forgot that he was meant to be taking wood to the mill. He lingered to join in the game of the holiday-makers' children, who were looking for slow-worms' nests. The tones of a violin rose, playing a lament, and it seemed that the trees were murmuring an accompaniment to the very human sound of its voice. The serving women squatting in their low huts prepared the coffee and they too sang a melancholy lamentation as they worked.

Coeddu was no longer thinking about either America or treasure when, all at once, he saw a tall man, whose dark face was surrounded by a bushy reddish beard, climbing up the slope followed by a black lamb and a white bitch.

'Uncle Mauro! Is that you?' he cried, running to meet him.

Yes, it was his uncle in person, whose sheepfold was not far from the little church and who was now bringing milk for the visitors. Uncle Mauro was a simple man: for here he was, aged fifty, and still a lowly farmhand; and also because, instead of scolding his nephew for being up here, he began to chat with the boy as if he were an adult, agreeing with him on the subject of going to America. He had never been beyond the environs of Nuoro either. Coeddu accompanied him back to his sheep fold, which consisted of a rough little hut made from branches. He saw through the trees what looked like a low black and white wall, but all at once the wall broke up, dissolved, changed place: it was the sheep, which were sleeping in a huddle and now, in the cool of the evening, woke up and spread out to graze.

Coeddu, enchanted, sat outside the hut while the little black lamb sucked at the bitch's teats, and uncle Mauro told the story of a bandit who wore round his neck a coin from Old Testament times, possibly even from Jesus's, and because of it had never been hit by a hostile bullet and never been a victim of fevers or carbuncles.

All this wove such a spell round Coeddu that he ended up drifting off to sleep. Even in his slumbers he could still see the moon descending on the horizon, as pink as a lump of coral, still hear the violin, far, far away, like the voice of a fairy. He could make out the noises of the sheep browsing, the creaking of the asphodel stems being crushed between their teeth. And over it all he could hear the gentle and monotonous music of their bells, like the clinking of crystal glasses tapped with a knife.

The following day the beggar children, who had returned down the mountain to Nuoro the previous evening, told him: 'Your mother's as mad as a boar. As soon as you get back she's sending you to America.'

'And I'm staying up here!' he replied.

The serving woman, a Good Samaritan, sent him to fetch milk, water, firewood, whilst she was instructing a novice cook. And in reward Coeddu received enormous plates of macaroni, of risotto, left-overs of partridge and tails and heads of trout, pears that were beginning to go off, cucumbers and tomatoes seasoned with oil, vinegar, pepper and salt. One evening he had terrible stomach pains and dreamed that a dog was eating his entrails. He didn't know why he felt sad: the young beggar boys took pleasure in tormenting him, bringing him dreadful messages from his mother. And to please the poor woman he decided to gather his courage and go looking for treasure. So one day he took uncle Mauro's axe and began to wander through the forest, stopping now and again to poke about between the tall and lonely rocks, knocking the iron head against the granite, which sometimes rang like crystal. In this way he arrived at a solitary and fearsome spot where the rocks had strange shapes: horses with human heads, frogs, fish, serpents. The silence surrounding them made them all the more mysterious. To give himself courage, he tried to imitate the cry and the wing-flapping of a crow; it didn't work; a few real crows answered, but instead of cheering him up, he felt his terror deepen. Nevertheless, he carried on, recognising the spot where, according to Uncle Mauro's account, an old shepherd had found a treasure, a heap of gold coins which the fortunate man, mad with joy, had hurriedly wrapped tightly inside his neckerchief, crying: 'Well, by the Devil, this time I'm rich!'

But immediately, inside the neckerchief the coins had turned into lumps of coal!

Coeddu, however, who had made up his mind not to speak a word and especially not to invoke the devil, who when he hears his name spoken transmutes gold into coal, walked on cautiously, silently. Besides, he was scared of the snakes, who have silver tails that whip and slash the face of anyone who disturbs them.

Rocks and more rocks. Between the twisted trees which resembled hundred-armed monsters, could be seen the sea, and the mountains of Oliena appeared as bluish snow. But all at once the horizon closed in. It seemed to the boy that he was suddenly in an enclosed courtyard encircled by cyclopean walls, and the sky, far above, seemed an intenser blue, almost dark like at evenfall. Here and there among the rocks there seemed to open great deep holes, and from one of these, unexpectedly, came a whistle like that of a train rushing from a tunnel. An icy sweat, a mortal pallor covered Coeddu's face. He sat down with a bump on a stone and squeezed his lips together to stop himself from crying out. It seemed to him the huge wall of rocks was moving round him in a strange way, and that the sky was turning ever darker. He felt dizzy, he raised his eyes and saw three naked giants leaping from rock to rock and coming closer to him. Then he gave a shout and fainted.

Uncle Mauro found him up there, stretched on the ground

as if dead. He carried him to his sheepfold, then down to the village, and a priest was summoned, who read the Gospel to drive out the phantasms that were tormenting the unhappy boy. But he remained delirious and continued to talk of giants and devils. Then a woman was summoned, who poured seven drops of lentisk oil and crumbled seven small pieces of clinker into a glass and having thus mixed the "water of terror" made the patient drink it: the patient was sick but continued to rave. Finally the doctor was summoned. 'It's a severe gastric episode,' he said: and he ordered Coeddu to take three purges.

The years have slipped by. Coeddu found his treasure without further searching, because his father sent him three thousand lire from America and he has bought forty sheep and a dog. Now he is fifteen and is more keen than ever not to leave his native mountain, convinced that he has seen a sight no longer seen even were one to circle the whole world: giants.

I saw him again a few days ago: sitting on the stones at the entrance to his "*tanca*", his extensive sheep enclosure, he was eating his barley bread and watching the sheep graze.

In the peacefulness of dusk the horizontal light was reflected in his eyes; his teeth gleamed like the leaves of the holm-oaks, his diminutive figure, all grey and black, merged with the background landscape, among the granite rocks and the dark tree trunks. He seemed to form, like this, a part of the place itself, solitary and majestic; and when he recounted his adventure I was tempted to believe him. Who knows? Perhaps giants really do exist, in the mysterious world of the mountains. It is they who pile the rocks together and cultivate the oak forests, keeping them luxuriant and fresh. But we, inhabitants of the city, do not see them because they hide when we appear. Perhaps they are as scared of us as we are of them.

CHECCA'S STORY

This is the third time already that Miss Checca has tried to run away from home. While she has lived with us, a member of the family, she has seemed powerfully attached to household affairs: she turns up here, she turns up there, she runs from one person to another, full of curiosity and good spirits, she sings, she permits her head to be scratched and she is, in short, our consolation. But as soon as she is left by herself, and perhaps because she has a compelling need for company, she goes down into the garden, hops on to the railings and flutters down into the street, running the risk of falling into the claws of her sworn enemy, the cat.

Because, you have already guessed, Miss Checca is a magpie.

She is a true magpie, a genuine wild bird, born in a wood on the edge of a marsh. A hunter took her from the nest, and after clipping her wings and tail, carried her off to a family we are friendly with. But if she didn't yet know how to fly, this young magpie, she already knew how to peck. The family's warm welcome was greeted with volleys of sharp pecks, and when they made contact, they hurt.

As a result, the cook began to harbour hostile feelings, especially since the bird's designated living quarters were in the kitchen, whose floor, thanks to Checca, was quickly decorated with droppings similar to little spots of cream. So the cook armed herself with a broom, and between the broom and the magpie there began a hellish battle. The poor bird pecked at its insensible enemy, hopping and fluttering in a desperate dance. The broom, in the cook's hands, was stronger than she was, and gave her an uncomfortable quarter of an hour.

Even now, when she sees a broom, Checca flaps her wings and flees in terror, and perhaps believes it to be a living thing, a cruel monster. And to this day she is unaware that the cook put this dilemma before her mistress: 'Either that bird goes, or I do.'

That is how she came to be a member of our household.

In our house there are no children. The times are too hard and money too scarce to be able to afford children. We thought of borrowing one, from time to time; in particular, we were often lent a little girl already mentioned in this book, a certain Mirella. But this Mirella goes to school now and studies incessantly, and you can't enliven a house every day without children. What are you to do? You try to forget, and in the same way that chicory becomes a substitute for coffee, so the little creatures made by the good Lord, the birds and cats, take the place of children.

Checca was the chosen one.

The day she came to our house, everyone gathered round her, competing to offer her breadcrumbs and stroke her head. She accepted the first and to the second she responded with angry squawks and pecks. For this she received no ill treatment, but was carried straight to the garden, set on the branch of a low tree, and while she gazed in wonderment at the sun and her eyes, previously green with rage, now turned blue again, we thought about how we could make her a little house of her own in that same tree, so she could imagine herself back in her native woods.

It was a long to-do, with all sorts of bothers, big and small. The whole range of vital tools, saws, billhooks, hammer, pincers, nails, etcetera, was assembled, along with planks and canes, for its construction. Very soon the open part of the garden was transformed into a work site. By happy chance a certain *signore* Lello became involved, a master carpenter expert in all things wooden, and thus, by the grace of God, the little house with its clever roof, and a horizontal pole inside for the magpie to perch on, and a platform outside for the feeding dish and water bowl, was completed. It was lashed in place in the branches of the tree, furnished with seeds and breadcrumbs; but the magpie refused to enter and still has not set foot in it today.

And yet, when she wants, she is the most intelligent and domesticated bird that can be imagined. She likes being in the house and everything interests her. She wants to see everything and poke her beak into everything. (Now I understand the meaning of this expression, which we clearly owe to some wise old man who has lived in the company of a magpie or a crow.)

She willingly comes to perch on your arm, and lets you stroke her, as soft and compliant as a little black dove. But she can scarcely stretch her neck in pleasure before her beak makes a stab at the first button she sees and won't let go, unless it's to open for the invisible passing of some insect, or the appearance of the cat.

With the cat, they pretend not even to see each other: one turns its head this way, the other that. But they only have to meet when no one is watching for a deadly quarrel to break out. If no one intervenes in time, there follows the most appalling tragedy ever recorded in the history of cats and magpies.

Everyone wishes her well, and when she is perched on the railing of the terrace, the children in the street call her and covet her.

'Checca, Checca! Oh, pretty Checca!'

She answers, turning this way and that, and sings for sheer pleasure, copying the songs of the other birds and calling back her own name as well. But her greatest pleasure is having a bath. She sits with her claws clamped tight on the rim of the wash tub, has a drink first of all, raising her head at every gulp so that she seems to be observing the water run down the gleaming feathers of her throat. Then she immerses her beak fully in the water and shakes it: the feathers on her head are soaked and stand on end. The game then continues, the beak dipping and shaking, sprinkling water over her breast, her wings and finally her tail, until all are thoroughly soaked. When she feels sufficiently drenched, she makes her way back to the terrace railings, in the sun, with her head tuft as erect as a Redskin warrior's, and completes her toilet by pecking at the feathers under her wings.

And to show how ardently she loves both cleanliness and the tranquil life, every now and again she opens her beak and swallows up annoying flies.

With all this, treated well, caressed, introduced to persons of good standing, protected from the cold, from rain, from street urchins who make attempts on her liberty, she can hardly want to escape.

Then, one morning, she thought it would be a good idea to fly down from the tree and go off to see the world. She was attracted by the cries of the street vendors opposite the garden. She must have thought: 'There are merry-sounding people down there, and I enjoy good company.'

Indeed, arriving via her quick fluttering mode of flight on the railing overlooking the market, she saw the women on the grocers' stalls, dressed in all manner of colourful materials, smelled the tang of cheese and cuts of lamb, and it seemed as if a fair was under way in the street below.

Everyone was cheerful, everyone was shouting as if in sport.

The fishmonger was shouting: 'The boat's in, all the fish freshly caught this morning. The boat's in.'

And the woman selling eggs: 'Eggs, eggs, twelve ha'pence apiece. They're not eggs, they're balloons. You'd need a boat to take one away: balloons, balloons.'

The cut-price man was declaring: 'Eight lire, eight lire only, bargain price. Roll up, roll up. Lovely, they are'

But the fishmonger insisted: 'Clear off, cheap-jack! Everyone's coming to me. The boat's come in.'

Checca, giddy and reckless, hopped down on to the pavement. Perhaps she imagined she was going to frisk about and enjoy herself as she did in our kitchen. But she had barely touched the ground before an urchin had already grabbed her by the wings, and in spite of her squawks and pecks carried her off at top speed, followed by a gang of his companions.

He took her back to his own home, a sad home in a dark room full of people who not only do not love the good Lord's birds but do not even love themselves.

'Is it good to eat?' an old hag asked the boy, making as if to wring Checca's neck.

And the urchin, to save the magpie, carried it down to a cellar, tied its leg with a piece of twine, and put out some fat grains of corn for it to eat. Checca was not used to this treatment. Tired of squawking and pecking, she became dejected and hid herself away in a corner, as far as the twine would let her. Once left on her own, she began to peck at the wall, as much for something to do, and made a small cavity, and then, worn out, with her foot bleeding from the tightly knotted string, she thought that perhaps it was all over for her. She pulled the damaged leg up into her feathers and stood motionless on the good leg, closed her eyes and went to sleep.

As luck would have it, the urchin's envious companions had been spying on him. After a long search, Checca was found and taken back home. She received a good scolding, much petting and plenty of soft breadcrumbs. All the next day she remained in a bad mood, bewildered, her eyes green, as when she is in the shadows. Doubtless she was remembering and repenting; then she returned to being cheerful, to poking her beak into the doings of the household, to singing and making fun of the other birds less strong and less fortunate than herself.

Until, left alone again, she ran away for a second time.

But we shall talk of this new adventure another day.

MY GODFATHER

The best man I ever knew in all the world was my godfather: and he could not have been anything else, considering that he was my father's closest friend.

My father, it could be said, never left the house, yet he knew, or was known by, an enormous number of people. Friends from distant villages came to seek him out and wish him well. Many of them, it is true, were seeking his help more than anything else, but there were some who were happy simply to be in his company. He never sought people out himself: but he loved and helped all those who turned to him.

This godfather of mine used to visit him from a village which at that time was a long way off, because mechanised transport had not yet carved its way into the harsh solitude of the Sardinian interior.

He used to come on horseback, slowly and peaceably, but he appeared to have flown, so vigorous and fresh was his face. His pure, soft beard seemed to retain a reflection of the white clouds that wandered over Mount Gonare, and his eyes shone with the placid calm of the new moon.

On his arrival, my mother told the maid: 'Light all the stoves.'

And the stove in every room was lit, just as for the solemn festivals. My father would lead his friend down to the cellar, from which they re-emerged laughing like children.

After dinner the two of them remained alone at table, with the bottle, which nodded in greeting now towards one, now towards the other, then straightened and appeared to be listening to their discussions, interrupting them again with its nodding gestures when these hinted at turning melancholy.

Even the saddest matters must have been discussed with serene good humour that night: the two friends took turns to tell each other their worries and made a point of not dwelling on them: they were able to shrug them off and forget them.

The cock's crow put a stop to their stories. And even the bottle no longer nodded, because it had neither the strength nor the will: it was empty.

On one of those nights, the maid went to fetch my little grandmother. The two of them went up to my mother's bedroom together and shortly afterwards the maid came down again and sought out the two friends. She said: 'Master, the mistress sends to tell you the stork has brought her a baby girl, just now, a few minutes ago.'

'Why didn't you warn me?' my father rebuked her.

'Because the mistress didn't want to disturb you when you had company.'

My father went up to see for himself: a baby girl, only just wrapped in its swaddling cloth, lay in a wicker basket beside the lighted fireplace: it did indeed seem that the stork had only just made its delivery.

The friend asked permission to see her as well: and my father said: 'This is an excellent opportunity for us to become relations. You can be her godfather.'

'Splendid; and what shall we call her?'

'We shall call her Grazia.'

And thus the guest became my godfather.

It was many years later that I heard him relate how all this had come about.

During my infancy I took little notice of my godfather. His visits interested me only for the fact that he would bring nice presents of fruit and sweetmeats.

On one occasion he brought me a little mouflon — a mountain sheep; and all the great air of the outdoors and the mountains, and the mysterious restlessness of the forests, entered the house along with the graceful animal, which was still in its wild state but timid and docile out of natural goodness.

All the other domesticated animals that populated the Noah's Ark that was our yard scented on the mouflon the native air of the high scrubland and its rocky lairs. They all gathered round him, therefore, to greet him. But the mouflon was scared, even of the hares, and in a single bound was on top of the wood-store as if on a mountain ledge. And it took the patience and agility of my godfather to persuade him to descend once more to the plain.

It was on this occasion, too, while we were sitting at table, that he related one of his travel adventures.

'My visit this time, dear fellow-parents, was not simply for the pleasure of seeing you and bringing you greetings. I left my home behind because for a number of days I had been tormented by a terrible toothache. I tried every remedy: rinses, compresses, hot cures and cold cures, prayers, entreaties: in vain. I was suffering so much that for the first time ever I sinned against the Lord's will: I wanted to die. Finally my wife said: Go to Nuoro, there must be a dentist there. And off I go. Usually I enjoy travelling, seeing the state of the fields, hearing the birds sing. This time I don't see a thing, I don't hear a thing, the pain is too great. I proceed as if through a fog. And all at once, under the shadow of Mount Gonare, what do I see looming up, as if really from a fog, but three rough-looking Christians, so rough they look like the Jews who slew Jesus in the Bible. And they're ready to slay me too, unless I instantly hand over the money and anything else I have on me. They want the horse as well. Take it all, just take it, dear brothers, and God help you. So they make me dismount and strip me of everything, like Christ: and there I'm left, all alone with the mouflon, which had prudently hidden behind a rock. There I am, alone and destitute; but what's this? The world seems changed. I see the meadows in flower, I hear the skylark, and I have the impression I've met, not the three highwaymen, but Saint Francis in person. You see, the thing is, the toothache has gone. All that agitation has removed it from my mouth better than the dentist could have done. And all blessings, therefore, on the three worthy men.'

He was speaking seriously. With his little white beard and his placid face he looked like Saint Francis in person.

THE THIEVES

The fearsome band comprised five individuals, three male and two female, and, it seems impossible but it is nevertheless the case, the leader was the bigger of these last two.

It is true that she was also the oldest and wiliest of the gang. It was she who assembled them, one day, in the meadows behind the Polyclinic, the very spot where for some time the most dreadful rogues have gathered and the most dastardly crimes have taken place. And she indicated the objective of their next expedition.

'We go down from here, along the new street where they're building those cottages. In one of those there's a doctor who's never at home. In the garden there are masses of roses, beans and artichokes. You, Gigetto, will climb the railings and open the gate. We go in: you two, Mario and Assunta, pick the flowers and the beans, and if there's time the artichokes; I

93

collect them up.'

'And then you run off, yes?' said Mario, jabbing a finger in her face.

'You just watch you don't blind me, right? Or I'll gouge your eyes out too,' she shouted, stepping back. 'And how can I run off with this kid on my back?' And she shook — as if keen to hurl him at her colleague Mario - the smallest member of the company, a baby boy little more than a year old, whom she was holding in her arms.

Gigetto spoke up. Gigetto always had his hands thrust in the pockets of his britches, although the pockets had great holes in them: he had aspirations of being the leader of the expedition himself.

'Leave it to me, Concetta. You're eight and a half and I'm eight: and eight in males is the same as ten in females. I know where this place is too; I know better than you. I've already been in: you can get in over the back wall. There's peas as well but they take too long to pick. So this is what we do…'

'No, we do as I say; otherwise I'm not coming,' said the scorned captain.

'If you don't want to come, all the better. That way the stuff will be all ours.'

'We'll see about that,' Concetta shouted, rushing at him. The other two began to yell as well, and the poor little baby was very nearly crushed in the middle of the brawl.

Then, once emotions had calmed, the expedition proceeded as planned, and even involved a piece of cunning tactics. Assunta and Concetta went ahead, with the baby of course, who clung to his sister's shoulder as if perched at a window from where everything appeared beautiful and interesting.

Suddenly, however, when they came to the new street where a number of cottages were under construction and others already completed, he began to scream.

'This is all I need,'Concetta said, her mind on other matters; and at first she tried to calm him gently, then she rained blows on him; finally she pulled from her pocket two unripe cherries and dangled them in front of his face. He immediately fell quiet and opened his mouth like a bird in a nest opening its beak.

In this fashion they arrived at the gate of the garden selected for their exploit.

The place did indeed seem uninhabited: windows of the house closed, garden deserted. The roses and bean plants swayed in the gentle west wind, as if greeting the girls, inviting them in. The artichokes were more haughty and austere, standing aloof on their tall stalks, afraid of nothing. There were also green asparagus with purple tips; but the two girls took no notice of these because they had never tasted asparagus.

Soon joined by the two males, they all marshalled themselves along the railings, studying the best way to break in. Even Gigetto was now of a mind to scale the gate, open it and let the gang into the garden. Everyone would work on their own account and then when the booty was all gathered together, it would be divided up. He, meanwhile, had provided himself with a pair of shears, which hung like a dagger from the rope that served him as a belt, and was eyeing the artichokes like a hostile tribe to be exterminated.

Mario, more gentle and dreamy, was thinking of the peas, so sweet and difficult to gather; blonde little Assunta was looking with desire at the roses, whilst Concetta, impartially savage, would willingly have laid her hands on everything.

When they were certain that no one could see them, Gigetto attacked the bars of the gate. He wriggled up it like a worm and his companions watched him in admiration spring down on the other side and drop right in front of them. Fortune came to their aid: the gate was not locked and seemed to open all by itself, in complicit silence.

The first to enter was Concetta, so sure of herself that she put the infant down, on the gravel of the drive, a situation he immediately accepted, playing with the little stones and his two unripe cherries.

In no time at all the garden was laid to waste: Gigetto cleverly cut off the artichokes at the base of their stems to make them into bunches; Mario pulled the pea plants out entirely and Assunta, with her hands bleeding from the thorns, broke off all the stems of roses. The greedy Concetta ran hither and thither like a wolf, grabbing everything she could; her petticoat, held up, served as a bag and grew ever fuller.

Even the cats, taking a beatific siesta under the tropical foliage of the artichoke plants, sprang up in terror and fled. Only the kindly roses and the dull beans continued to nod and bow in the breeze as if the disaster was of no concern to them.

God, however, is on the watch for all misdeeds.

Suddenly a window opened, a fearsome face appeared,

with a black beard and two fiery eyes, and a voice thundered: 'Put everything down, you scoundrels. Put it down now, or you'll be shot.'

Another window opened: the voice of a witch cried: 'Stay where you are, stay where you are, I'm coming for you now, you rabble!'

The thieves took to their heels, leaving their booty behind.

And when the doctor came rushing down he found only the little baby boy, abandoned on the gravel in the drive.

'Who are you? What is your name?' he yelled.

The infant turned up to him his two eyes, deep blue like a crow's, then showed him his two half eaten cherries; finally he stretched out his little hands because he wanted to be helped to stand up.

And the doctor began to laugh. Then he had to send the maid to run after the thieves to give them back the poor little mite.

AS YOU SOW, SO SHALL YOU REAP

Mimmo and Momo had decided to run away to America. And they wanted to run away not as a result of reading books of adventure, but because the pair of them, who had fought and argued with each other since birth, were agreed on one thing alone: a hatred of books.

Sons of peasants who had grown rich, they had been sent to school and it was intended that they should become doctors, or better still, vets or chemists. And while they were at infants' and elementary schools, the plan went very well. They had nothing more serious to think about than entertaining themselves. The two children lived out in the country, in a large farmhouse, and to get to school they had to follow a long road between two broad ditches of running water, like two rivers. Vines and fields and trees on both sides; nests, frogs, birds and all kinds of small creatures. And then their friends, and their adversaries from the neighbouring village; and the inn halfway along the road, where everything could be had: toffees, dried figs, dried chestnuts, bread sticks, a warming fire in winter and ice cream in summer.

This road, then, was the veritable highway to earthly paradise. Often their bags, full of books rendered even more stupid by the joys of winter frosts or summer suns, ended up hurled into the grass like the victims of satchel-murderers.

In winter, unlikely as it may seem, the entertainments were greater. They could stop and wait for the *caladon*, the primitive snow-clearing machine, with its eight steaming oxen, to carve a path through the snow-covered road. And when the operation was about to begin, the children threw themselves behind the heavy triangular device, all gleaming iron chains, pretending it was they who were pushing its pointed nose forwards. Then came the bicycle age. Momo and Mimmo had two identical ones, costing eight hundred lire each. The parents did not flinch at the expense, since their sons were to become doctors or, let us hope, vets or chemists.

But the good times were now at an end. Having learnt by heart "The tree to which you used to stretch your little baby hand", they had to turn their attention to Latin. And Mimmo and Momo had to go to secondary school. It could have been a grand school in a great city like London or Rome, or like Parma at least. No, this was the school at Casalmaggiore, from whose windows the farmers could be seen going to market, and in the distance the fields cultivated by their own parents and the highway to paradise now forever lost.

It was for this reason that the two brothers had decided to

run away to America.

They wanted to work on the land, like their fathers, like their forefathers, and the forefathers of the forefathers, all the way back to *signore* Adam, the man who had indeed been driven from the earthly paradise and had then earned his daily bread by the sweat of his brow.

'We'll sell the bikes, to the mechanic who owns the shop opposite the school. Then we'll take the train, and away we'll go.' Mimmo said. And his little red mouth closed on a shiny whistle which looked like a star flashing across the night sky of August.

Momo was younger but more practical. It was he who thought about the basket of provisions and the initial expenses of the journey.

Here it should be mentioned that in the farmers' houses, there was a supply of almost everything. Certain items, however, since olives, coffee plants, as well as cotton and castor oil, did not thrive in the surrounding fields, and the salt marshes and sugar refineries and paraffin factories were somewhat distant, certain items, therefore, it would be necessary to buy in the village. And since the women never left the house and the men were occupied in the fields, the two small boys took the task upon themselves. Momo especially was skilful at bargaining, and attentive to the last centime.

From the handlebars of his bicycle there constantly hung a basket, which left home empty each day and returned full. He often brought bread as well, because their home-made bread was too hard for the teeth of guests; and they constantly had guests in the house.

And then one day the two boys' grandmother, who was a

notably tight-fisted woman, and often didn't sleep at night out of concern over the high and ever-increasing cost of living, came close to having a heart attack when Momo informed her that the price of bread had gone up. It had gone up by ten *soldi* a kilo, no less. And even salt cost double what it did before.

'If this is how it starts, God knows where it will end. Bread? Salt? But then everything else will go up dreadfully.'

'Exactly, grandma, exactly. You were right yesterday, grandma,' Momo said the next day, thoughtful and preoccupied. 'Everything has gone up: coffee, sugar, paraffin, wicks. Nails too: look, they now cost two *soldi* each. The very small ones!'

'God, God, where's it going to end? It'll bring on the revolution for sure.'

'Let's hope not, grandma, because the first to suffer will be us. Think, if they come here, the revolutionaries I mean, they'll take away our cows and our pigs. Have you thought of that?'

So the grandmother resigned herself. Better to pay high prices for salt than lose all the family holdings. And she handed over the coins with a sigh.

'You know, Mimmo,' Momo said to his brother, when it came to discussing seriously their planned flight, 'I've put aside nearly ninety lire these last few days, from the extra on the cost of things.'

Because, you'll have guessed, this worsening situation in the cost of living was entirely his own work.

Came the great day. The two brothers had already arranged the sale of the bicycles and retrieved from the haystack an old suitcase containing fresh linen, shoes, a salami sausage, two large pears, a metal tray to sell in America, shoe-polish, thread, needles, pliers. They had provided all these things for themselves, leaving at home, untouched, their school books and exercise books.

They hated the things so much, books, that they did not even consider consulting the railway timetables. After all, you can find out all you need to know at the stations, and by asking which road to take you can even get to the North Pole.

To avoid falling prey to emotion, or giving themselves away, they decided to leave without saying goodbye to anyone; just the dog, who, perhaps apprehending their intentions, followed them out to the road: they waved farewell to him. And that was all.

The mechanic with whom they had arranged the sale of the bicycles was waiting for them at the door of his shop, alongside the display window filled with mysterious and shiny objects.

He was a tall man, as tall as his door, with very long red moustaches, which reminded the more studious pupils at the school of the barbarian invasion of Italy under King Alboin and the similarly ferocious Lombards, whose moustaches must have been like this. The mechanic, on the contrary, was a good-natured fellow, a man of conscience, incapable of hurting a fly. So much so that on the question of agreeing a price for the bicycles, which he himself had sold them a year ago, he didn't quibble over a centime. The two brothers, already experts in business, asked seven hundred and fifty for each, and seven hundred and fifty for each the mechanic was prepared to pay.

Once this pair of nimble metallic steeds was inside

the shop, leaning one behind the other against the wall, the mechanic opened the drawer of his till and peered deeply inside.

The hearts of the two rogues beat with joy; the sweaty hand of Momo was already stretched out to take the money.

'But, boys,' the mechanic said in his pleasant baritone voice, 'wouldn't it be better if your father took the money? After all, he was the one who bought the bicycles.'

'Especially since I'm here already,' the boys' father said, springing from the back of the shop like a jack-in-the-box.

Here I should explain what you have already understood: the mechanic had warned the unfortunate father of the boys' depraved intentions. And the father, without wearying himself giving them a long lecture or even an admonitory word, took them each by a hand and conducted them to the school building. Which was a case of merely crossing the road.

The suitcase remained deposited with the mechanic.

When they were back in school, the two adventurers wept — in rage, that is — then, as soon as they were on their own, started to argue and fight all over again.

The mother also wept, when she learned of their ingratitude; the grandmother wept too. But the next day she took consolation in the discovery that the prices of bread and other essentials were on the way down in an impressive fashion.

THE GIRL FROM OTTANA

In the ancient village of Ottàna lived seven brothers — three dark, three fair and one albino — and all seven got on with each other so harmoniously that they were the envy of their neighbours and even their own relatives. Then one of these relatives, more envious than the others, invited a man known to be an enemy of the seven brothers to go hunting with him. He led him into a wood and there, while they were waiting for the moon to set and the boars to come down to drink at the pool, he killed the man and hid the body under a lentisk bush. The seven brothers were accused of this killing and had to run away and become outlaws to avoid being hanged like real murderers. But even in their troubles, they continued to look after each other, and when three of them slept, the other four kept watch. They roamed the countryside, through woods and forests, until they found shelter in an old *nuraghe* in the district of Goceano. This ancient stone chamber of the Nuraghe people was not only intact, but searching its dark corners the albino brother found stone arrowheads and knives, cork-wood vessels like the one the Sardinian shepherds still use and spoons made from sheep's toenails. The ancient edifice was encircled by a terrace of earthworks supported on large boulders. Ivy and lentisk grew between the stones of this mysterious refuge. This, then, was the place the seven brothers settled on for their new dwelling. From here, they set out early each morning to hunt, returned in the evening and ate. Then, while some of them kept watch from the platform around the building, like sentries on the sentry-walk of a fortress, the others, before going to sleep, told stories of the first inhabitants of the *nuraghi* and the albino brother maintained that these people had been the Atlantidi, the refugees from Atlanta who escaped to Sardinia when the ocean submerged their mysterious land. And when the senior brother related the legends he had heard from his grandmother concerning Sardus the Father* and the temple the original Sardinians had erected to him, the other brothers removed their caps and listened with religious attention. Each of them had round his neck, attached by a leather thong, a coin with an effigy of Sardus the Father, which preserved him from misfortune.

And then, one April afternoon, after spearing on seven spits seven pieces of boar's meat which they left beside the fire in the middle of the *nuraghe*, the seven brothers went off to hunt the stag. When they returned, towards evening, they found the boar's flesh already cooked, the fire still burning, the room tidied up, the terrace swept. One of the seven pieces of boar's flesh already cooked, however, was missing. The seven men looked at one another in wonderment. They searched all round the site but found no one. The next day they left beside the fire seven *cassadinas***, and when they returned they found only six, and the house tidied up and the terrace swept. So on the third day, one of the seven brothers, the albino one to be exact, stayed behind in the *nuraghe*, lying hidden beneath a sleeping-pallet. The other six brothers went off to hunt; and silence fell all around. Beside the fire, speared on the seven spits, seven *casizolos**** as yellow and fragrant as apples, were slowly cooking. From the entrance the April breeze, perfumed with mint and dog-rose, wafted into the hut. The sound of the rushing stream on Mount Rasu could be heard, and the songs of the nightingales in the oaks of the forest.

And so it happened that the albino brother was about to fall asleep in his hiding place when a faint rustle caught his attention: someone was sweeping the terrace, and after a moment a dark shadow obscured the entrance to the *nuraghe* and a faint sound of footsteps disturbed the silence of the room. Then he threw off the sleeping-pallet and saw a girl, small in stature, but so daintily made and so beautiful that at first he believed her to be a *jana*, a mountain fairy. But from the cry of fear she gave he realised she was a poor young girl. Or rather a real live girl from Ottàna. As would any other girl the world over in her circumstances, the girl from Ottàna knelt weeping at the feet of the albino brother, and explained that she was the niece of the envious man who had ruined the seven brothers.

'He took me in and brought me up, because I am an orphan. But now that I am fifteen, he wanted to marry me. I told him: no, I don't want to marry you because you are old. Then he sent me away to those woods down there with two servants, who had orders to kill me and bring back to him my heart and my eyes. When we reached the woods the two servants drew their knives but they didn't have the heart to kill me. When they didn't have the heart to kill me, they wandered through the wood for a while until they found a deer: they slaughtered it, cut out its heart and eyes and carried them back to my stone-hearted uncle. I remained in the woods and roamed the countryside until I found myself looking up at this *nuraghe*. I went in and took the meat and swept the terrace. Now here I am again. Kill me likewise, if you want to, but don't reveal to my stone-hearted uncle that I am alive.'

The albino brother turned his head away so that the girl should not see he had tears in his eyes; then he shouted: 'Get up, and tell me your name.'

'Juannicca.'

He shouted, louder still: 'Keep sweeping, and mend that pallet.'

So Juannicca rose and continued to work. And when dusk came, the other six brothers returned, dirty and muffled against the cold, they sat round the fire while the albino brother recounted the story of the girl Juannicca and the girl Juannicca, crouching at the back of the *nuraghe*, trembled like a frightened hare. But the senior brother said: 'Well, we are after all relatives in a way. You can keep house for us, you can keep the fire alight and fetch the water and we will consider you as our sister. But, I warn you, keep your tongue in your mouth.'

So Juannicca, keeping her tongue in her mouth, made no reply; and they were all of them pleased by her silence. And the days passed, and the seven brothers, when they returned to their refuge at the fall of evening, did not speak, but sighed, stared up at the stars glistening above the oak trees, and even smiled. All seven of them were in love with Juannicca; and one of them brought her in his pocket a bunch of early periwinkles, one a young hare seized from its form, one a coloured stone found by chance in the bed of the stream, perhaps fallen from the ring of some girl who was washing.

Juannicca smiled at all seven brothers, and when they were late returning in the evening she even went out on to the terrace and looked up at the seven stars of Ursa Major, standing brightly over the distant mountains, and it was as if she could see her seven protectors.

They began to argue, because each of them wanted to marry the girl. The senior brother wanted her because he was the senior of the brothers; the albino brother wanted her because he had been the one who saw her first; the others wanted her because they wanted her.

In the end, they decided not to marry her and to have her always with them as their sister. And thus time passed, winter passed, and the song of the cuckoo announced the return of the fine weather. Juannicca asked the cuckoo:

> *'Cuccu bellu 'e mare,*
> *'Cantos annos bi cheret a mi cojare ?'*

'Say, pretty cuckoo from o'er the sea,
'How many years 'til I married be?'

And the cuckoo responded with seven melancholy calls. But Juannicca shook her head, disbelieving, because she did not hope to be able to get married as quickly as that, in this lonely spot where there weren't even any marriage announcements in the newspapers.

And then one day, when she was out on the terrace, carding wool, whom should she see passing by but a young man on horseback out hunting.

He was tall and handsome, with long black hair flying behind like ribbons of black satin; and from under his thick eyebrows his black eyes shone like stars under the clouds. He greeted Juannicca, calling to her: 'What are you doing?'

'What it looks like!' she replied.

To stare at one another and to fall in love was one and the same thing.

He passed by again the next day, and was struck by the deftness with which the girl was now spinning the carded wool. On the third day he said to her: 'If you come with me, I will marry you. I am the son of the Prince of Logudoro. Climb up on my horse and let us go.'

'Come back later,' she said. 'First I want to clean the house. And then I will come only on the condition that you take a hand in overturning the judgement passed on my seven brothers.'

'By my conscience, I will do so.'

He returned later, and from the low wall surrounding the terrace she jumped up behind him, put an arm round his waist, and off they trotted.

It was a beautiful spring day: the greenish tips of the trees stood out against the little silvery clouds, and the flowering bushes, asphodel, laurel, thyme and broom, all added their perfumes to the air. Juannicca recounted her story and the hunter said: 'I have three sisters, Grassia, Itria and Baingia, pretty as three carnations. They will like you very much, and will teach you to embroider tapestry and play the guitar. But if they see you dressed like this, in those worn-out clothes, they will say: "Our brother's bride is a beggar girl." Therefore listen: I shall leave you in the wood, beneath the castle of Goceano, and I shall go and bring you a beautiful costume, and you will wait for me and never move from the spot.'

And soon there appeared before them the castle, perched like an eagle on the summit of a rocky hill. Lit by the sun, the spring clouds formed a golden aureole all around it; clusters of wild pear trees were in flower at the foot of the hill. The hunter said: 'Now, Juannicca, don't move. I'll bring you back a necklace too.'

She dismounted and sat down on a stone. But hardly had the young man disappeared from view than she heard the trilling of a nightingale and thought: 'There must be a stream there. I want to wash, I must not enter the castle all dirty like this.'

She rose to her feet and searched and searched but this stream would not be found. But suddenly a woman appeared in the path, tall and withered, with red hair and strange green eyes: she greeted Juannicca and asked her who she was and what she was looking for.

Juannicca had lived amongst good people for so many months that she had forgotten that there exist in this world bad people also. So she could never have imagined that this red-head was a sorceress in love with the young hunter, and did not hesitate to tell the woman her story.

'It would be useless to wash and to dress in fine clothes if your hair is left undone,' the woman said, controlling her rage. 'Come with me and let me arrange your hair. I will comb lentisk oil through it to make it shine and fix the scarf with a pin.' So she led her to a grotto, oiled her hair, arranged it in the style of a lady, bound her head in a scarf and fixed it in place with a silver pin. And the moment the woman inserted the pin, which was bewitched, Juannicca fell to the ground as if dead.

She fell to the ground as if dead and thus she remained for seven years.

The hunter, unable to find her, believed she must have regretted her decision to go with him and returned to the old stone dwelling; and because he thought it would be dishonourable to pursue her, he took no further steps. But the grief and humiliation made him taciturn and cold. He did not leave the castle and forbade his sisters to play or sing. When he became the Prince himself after a few years, he prohibited all festivals and had flatterers thrown in prison. Which shows that sometimes discontent makes men energetic and wise.

The sisters, however, grew bored. One day, going into the woods to gather asphodels to weave baskets, they began to speak ill of their brother, and their conversation became so animated that they missed the proper path. All at once it started to rain. The sisters took refuge in a grotto and saw, stretched out on the ground, a beautiful young girl who appeared to be dead. Her clothes were ragged, but her hair was arranged in the style of a lady, and the scarf fixed in place with a silver pin.

One of the sisters said: 'I want to see if this pin suits me.'

But hardly had she drawn it from the hair of the sleeping beauty than the girl woke up, and began to weep and to call for the hunter. Then the three sisters lifted her up and comforted her and took her with them to the castle. At first the young lord was very angry; then he married Juannicca, and when he had married Juannicca he had the judgement passed on the seven brothers overturned, and he became so happy that he smiled even when the flatterers told him the most foolish things in the world.

* Sardus the Father: the first man to colonise the island of Sardinia.

** *casadinas*: a kind of focaccia made from pasta and cheese.

*** *casizolos*: a semi-hard Brie-style cheese.

OLD MOISÈ

When I was a little girl, we had an old servant from the Barbagia called Moisè. Was it his real name? I don't think so. It may have been a nickname because the old man really did look like the prophet Moses, tall and brown-faced as he was, with a long curly beard. But more likely it was because among other things he knew how to conjure spells against the evil eye, against illnesses among the cattle, against the ants that carry off grain from the threshing floor, against caterpillars, locusts and maggots, against the eagles to prevent them from seizing little piglets, lambs, and even young children. And included in almost all of these exorcising spells (in dialect called *verbos*, that is, mysterious words) there was an invocation to Moses.

Moisè was old but still robust, and he worked all year round. In winter he watched over the herds of hogs and sows as they foraged and ate acorns, up among the holm-oak woods of Mount Orthobene. But he returned to the village for the great religious festivals, and especially Christmas, which he wanted to spend at his masters' house. He was far from being a decrepit old man, is what I mean, but to hear him speak you would think he was at least two thousand years old. All the stories he told were set in the olden days, those 'ancient times' when Jesus had not yet been born and the world was populated by simple folk and also by fantastical creatures, animals who spoke, devils, dwarves and *birghines*, virgins who were good with the good people and bad with the bad and spent their time weaving purple and gold.

When Moisè returned to the house for Christmas, we crowded round him to hear his stories. Initially, he had to be pleaded with and begged: he preferred to teach us how to roast acorns in the embers of the fire, which made them swell and turn red and become as good to eat as chestnuts. And he told us that in certain parts of Sardinia they even make bread with acorn flour, to which one adds a certain type of clay that improves its taste and consistency. Then, by dint of imploring looks and much entreaty, one could succeed in getting him to tell some stories.

Seated round the hearth, where whole sections of oak trunk were burning, or whole lentisk roots black and knotted like Medusas' heads, we would listen eagerly. It was still early for the great dinner which is eaten after returning from midnight Mass, at which we, however, were not present because on Christmas night the weather is almost always harsh and on harsh nights children have to go to bed; but for us and for all those who wanted to eat without profaning the Christmas Eve vigil, a special dish had been prepared of macaroni seasoned with a ground walnut sauce, and with this and with Moisè's stories we contented ourselves. So then he blew on the fire, using an iron rod: a hollow tube which was actually the barrel of an old arquebus, and began: 'When Jesus was born,' he said, 'people were still good and without malice. But just so: because men were simple-minded and afraid of everything, the world was infested with malign creatures. At that time wicked fairies existed, who could transform themselves into different animals and often got into people's houses as cats, dogs or hens and brought bad luck. At that time there existed green horses, which led their riders over precipices; and there were vampires, there were serpents and especially a terrible one called Cananèa. But above all, good shepherds and good housewives were plagued by devils who took on human shape and pretended to be shepherds themselves and could only be recognised by their curling nails or their feet like a donkey's. Jesus came into the world to free it from all these malign creatures, and especially from the devils. In fact they no longer exist nowadays. But before they vanished from the world, what did the devils and the malign creatures do? They left objects lying about, objects so impregnated with their malignity that the men who touched them became bad and passed their badness on to their descendants. There is no other explanation for the wickedness of certain men who really do seem like devils. Even the Jews who arrested and killed Jesus were men who had been corrupted by touching some of those objects left by the devil, and the bad children of our times are still called little devils. In any case, men still hold a great festival to remember the birth of Jesus, their liberator. With people who still live in patriarchal societies, like Sardinia's, the festival truly begins after midnight and goes on until dawn, with singing, playing, dancing, and continues all through the carnival. In certain villages the people bring things with them to eat in church, and after the Gloria they all start cracking walnuts and almonds; by dawn the church floor is covered in apple and orange peel and nut shells. In almost all the villages people exchange presents, and young men engaged to be married give the bride-to-be money in gold or silver coins, or send a young pig as a gift.

'When I was a boy, a curious thing happened to me.

'My father was a swineherd, and he lived out of doors all year round; but for Easter Day and Christmas Day he insisted on returning to his village. While I was little, he got a servant to look after the herd on those days. But as soon as I was old enough to help him, he took me to the pig enclosure, and on Christmas night left me to stay up there, in the cold, damp wood, in a hut or even in a cave sheltered from the winds and snow, yes, but dark and frightening like the grottos in the legends. I wasn't frightened, because my father said he was leaving me on my own on purpose, to get me used to being brave. But during that night, waiting for Christmas, I felt sad and dejected. I lay down in a corner, as soon as evening came, and covered myself with my cloak, long and wide and made of strips of *orbache*, the rough Sardinian wool cloth which we shepherds throw over our heads and shoulders in winter and tie under our chin. And I thought of Christmas in the village. I can see it, I thought: my sister's young man has already sent her a fine piglet with its nice red rind, its insides removed, and stuffed with bay leaves, my mother is already preparing the grand supper, while my sister is putting on her new clothes and adjusting her hood to go to Mass. The fiancé arrives, his pockets crammed with oranges, nuts, dried cherries; he summons his strength and leans to one side to haul out all these good things, he puts them on the bench beside the hearth and says: if only poor Moisè was here! Save this lovely quince for him, it looks like gold.

'Thinking of this valiant young man I felt moved. He came from a good family, but he could not yet marry my sister because, the way it was, his family didn't think it was right, what with him being too young and having his military service still to do. He was a cheerful fellow, a jester, with his pockets always full of dried fruits, and for this I liked him a lot. My father said that my sister's fiancé had more nuts in his pockets than he had farthings; but the way it was, I preferred him like this. He used to tell me terrible stories, about bandits, and green horses, and the Mother of the Winds, and I liked him because of that as well.

'On one occasion he came all the way up to the pigs' enclosure to find me, the day before Christmas Eve (my father must have gone down to the village at the end of that day) and he stayed until dusk telling me fables and scary little stories. He told me boys mustn't leave their houses when the winds are blowing, because, the way it is, the Mother of the Winds, who sweeps across the countryside with her sons, well, she carries off any passer-by who isn't strong and any creature who can't resist.

'Towards evening he went away. I remained alone, and even though the evening was calm, I was frightened to go out. I lay down under the cloak, and began to think of the next night's festival. I seemed to see the fiancé arriving, with his pockets full of fruit; the bells were ringing, the women were rocking their babies, singing:

> *'Su ninnicheddu,*
> *Non portat manteddu,*
> *Nemmancu curittu:*
> *In tempus di frittu*
> *No narat tittìa.*
> *Dormi, vida e coro,*
> *E reposa anninnia.'*

> 'The little child so beautiful,
> He has no coat of warming wool,
> Nor jacket snug round him to fold;
> When the season turns to cold
> He neither makes complaint nor cries.
> Sleep then, my life; sleep then, my heart,
> Wrapped in soothing lullabyes.'

'The people went to Mass; and I seemed to see the church lit by seven rows of candles and the altars adorned with orange branches laden with fruit. When they returned to the house everyone sat on the mats by the fireplace and the great dinner began. They feasted on piglet, the first curds of milk, cheese with honey; they drank, they laughed.

'Then the senior men, sitting cross-legged around the fire, improvised songs, and the young people danced the round-dance. It was the beginning of a celebration that lasted until first light, and everyone seemed mad with joy, everyone laughed and sang because Jesus was born and the devil was made to vanish from the earth.

'I was as sad as some wild creature all alone in the woods. I was eleven and it was already the third Christmas I had spent on the mountain. For me, childhood had ended all too quickly; yet I felt as nervous as a five-year-old. All at once I hear the hogs grunting in the enclosure, or rather in the pen of boulders where they were sheltering! A thief? The dog, however, a big dog that looked like a lion, tied to the trunk of a tree, wasn't barking. I remembered the instructions my father gave me. So I showed myself in the entrance of the hut, calling "Basile, Antoni, Sarbadore" to make the thief think there were lots of people with me and make him run away. Then the dog began to bark as well, and it seemed to be speaking to someone, accusing him. But as for me, even if I wasn't frightened of the thief, I thought again of the stories my sister's fiancé had told me, and I didn't dare go any further.

'It was a cold but clear night. The moon was rising into a silvery sky and you could just make things out, as if it was dawn. I summoned up my courage, took the old arquebus, which was twice my size, and went out into the clearing. But suddenly I thought I saw not far from me a group of pigs being led by a dark, thick-set man. Then I remembered that in olden times, before men became malicious, the devil used to pasture at night the souls of the wicked who had been transformed into wild boars, and I ran back to hide in the hut, full of fear. I couldn't help it. I too had no sense of evil in me, at that time, like the men of olden times. The sense of evil came to me two days later, when my father returned, counted the hogs and finding one missing beat me. Out of shame I didn't tell him anything, neither about the fiancé's visit nor his scary stories, nor of the noise I had heard in the night, nor of my superstitious terror. He believed I had allowed the young hog to wander off and get lost in the forest, and that was what he beat me for. If he had known of my fear and my foolish terror, he would have beaten me all the same and made fun of me into the bargain.

'But the person who did begin to make fun of me, after that time, was my sister's fiancé. Even he knew only half the story, and he couldn't admit to knowing that. And only years and years later, when he had become a serious grown-up and I a young man full of evil ways, did everyone know the secret of that night. The young hog had been stolen by him, the fiancé, because he didn't have enough money to buy one; and the next day he had given it to his bride-to-be, my sister. He had come up to visit me on purpose, to tell me those frightening stories, and stop me from leaving the hut at night. My father, who by that time was an elderly and peaceable man, a patriarch, turned scarlet with anger when he heard this tale, thinking that he had eaten his own stolen pig. And he tried to get up off his mat to run after me and beat me again!'

FISHING
(A STORY FOR SLIGHTLY BIGGER PEOPLE)

The two friends' little stroll along the beach was halted by
the obstacle of a thick rope which a number of fishermen
were hauling from the sea. One behind the other, a few paces
apart, they were edging backwards, arms and spines straining,
towards the sandy ridge at the top of the beach.

Each of them had a kind of rope harness round his chest,
fastened by a wooden pin at the front in such a way as not
to press on his stomach; and tied to the pin a short length of
rope, a sort of cord with a hook on the end, which helped the
fisherman's hand get a better grip and pull on the cable with
more power.

This harness was the sign that all of them, old men,
young men, children, and a woman who appeared to be made
of sand — and she too was pulling vigorously — belonged

to the community of the ancient black boat, like Saint Peter the Apostle's, which was dawdling in the water just offshore, abandoned to its own devices, while the little blue waves lapped round it.

The rope was never-ending: the sea seemed to be full of it. They pulled and pulled, and when the fisherman at the end of the line reached the top of the bank, he dropped it on the sand and ran to catch hold of it again at the shoreline, the hook on its cord ringing like a small bell; and so it went on.

Some metres away to the side, the same process was being mirrored. Another cable, in other words, was being drawn from the sea, hauled up to the ridge, dropped on the pile that had already formed at the back of the beach; and the pullers came and went in rotation, giving the effect that there were more of them than there actually were, like walk-ons in the theatre scurrying about to represent a crowd.

These people had all the features of the common crowd too: a mixture of old, young, boys and small children, all of them rough-looking and sunburnt, with the dry, gnarled appearance of salted fish, yet each one different from the next. They were dressed in every imaginable sort of rag, their legs bare though, and their feet like briar roots, and on their heads, caps, hats and headgear suggestive of the entire range of mushrooms, both edible and poisonous. Even the woman had a yellow headscarf, worn in such a way that her head looked like a lemon.

'But what are they doing?' asked the smaller of the two friends.

The larger would have had no more idea himself if he had not once been part of the operation: so he gave a display of erudition.

'It's bottom fishing, that's what the net's called that's down there in the water where you can't see it. A bottom net means a net lying on the sand, because it's not used in deep water. This sort of fishing is also called drag fishing, because you can see how they're pulling.'

'Oh, yes, I can see that,' the other agreed, and watched enchanted.

And into his mind came the image of his parents, who argued all the time, or at least complained, over the lack of money, the difficulties of life and the hardships of daily work. Even now, when they were staying here for a fortnight's rest, on account of him, Matteino, who absolutely had to have some sea air, even now they could find no peace. Less than before, in fact, because their funds, the mother said, disappeared as if carried off by the wind, and the father replied that she was the one at fault because she didn't know how to economise. But how can one economise when bread costs more than tarts once did, and *pomidoro*, or apples of gold to give tomatoes their proper name, were sold at prices suggesting their name was literal, and for a tiny fish, damn their poverty, (when she is exasperated the mother uses the language of the women in the market), they make you fork out as if it's got a pearl in its belly.

Whereas everyone knows how many fish, in comparison, these fishermen, who resemble nothing so much as gypsies of the sea, eat for themselves in peace and happiness.

Happy, at this moment, they do not in truth appear to be, and not even at peace, because they too are quarrelling, one with another on the same rope, or across the space with the people on the other rope. And there are shouts, curses, insults, of which the most delicate are "dirty thief" or "son of a dog", and they would perhaps set to with their fists if the fists, stiff and burning, were not, on their own independent account, concentrating on hauling on the cable.

And the cable, as rust-red and greasy as a hard sausage, willingly lets itself be hauled, even giving the impression of being the one hauling from the sea the mysterious weight of the still invisible net.

A few boys who have come to swim, but have been watching the spectacle for a long time, out of a pure spirit of human solidarity, or because they believe their able-bodied assistance might speed the operation up, interpose themselves between the fishermen and start to pull as well. A gentleman in a singlet and a sailor's cap adds himself to their number, a fine specimen of the slave-dealer type with teeth, even the front ones, of gold. A spinsterish-looking woman, dressed in green like a grasshopper, joins in too.

'Well done, good for you,' come the shouts from all round.

'But the fish they're fishing for, who gets them?' Matteino asks his friend.

'They sell them, or if there aren't many, they share them out between them. Even I got some once because I helped pull them in.'

Then a brilliant idea swims into Matteino's head: join the rope and pull too, and then take back to his overworked mother his bathing cap filled with fish.

'Let's pull too,' he proposed to his friend. But the friend pulled a face, first of all because Matteino was so small and frail he looked as if he was made of matchsticks, then because that time he did help pull, he gave himself blisters on his hands and the cook threw away the fish he brought home, which had not, as he claimed, been given to him by the miserly fishermen but picked up from ones they had rejected and left on the beach.

Meanwhile, among the lapping blue waves which seemed to be graciously lending a hand in bringing the net to shore, the first signs of it could already be seen with the appearance of cork floats on the surface. The fishermen now fell silent, pulling with more strength, their faces brightening with hope. The sandy woman was the most animated of all. When it came to her turn to drop the rope and go back to the shoreline, she rushed down from the ridge and seized the cable once more, throwing herself backwards on her harness as if her whole life depended on that one effort.

It was behind her, in the gap between her and a ruddy man whose sweat seemed like blood, that Matteino, caught up in the general atmosphere of hope, set himself to pull on the rope. And he felt it was up to him alone to supply the necessary strength still required to bring the operation to completion.

'Strength, courage, pull, pull,' Matteino said to himself, in a state of intoxication that made him forget the feeble effect of his contribution. Up, up, the sand seemed to slip from under his feet, and in truth he felt he was being carried, between the muscular man and the determined woman, as if suspended in the air.

The net could now be seen, coming very slowly from the sea's embrace. It resembled a giant basket of red gauze trimmed with knots of cork and pierced by splinters of steel. They were the first tiny fish, which aroused in Matteino a feeling of pity. Poor, poor little fish! They were calmly swimming and looking through the little windows of the net because it was still full of water. But once they were on the beach, and realised the horror of their fate, they began to wriggle and turn somersaults, bending themselves double like silver rings, and some of them managing to leap out of their prison.

'But if these ones here are the whole catch, we're in a fix,' Matteino thinks, and at the same time sees the diabolical face of his friend creased in a mocking sneer. The fishermen on the other hand were all alight with a silent joy. Their faces were glowing as if the sun was just rising from the sea. They could feel the weight of the net; the woman was feeling it more than anyone, for under the arch of her yellow headscarf her amber eyes were shining like those of a hunting dog.

Even the sturdy slave-dealer, with his gold teeth, was smiling in satisfaction, as if he had been the owner of the catch.

A crowd of curious bystanders had now gathered all along the two ropes, like a crowd held back along the line of a royal procession. Others were coming, and one could see the long pink legs of half-bare women seemingly dancing across the blue background of the sea.

'Land them, land them,' one little ragamuffin shouted.

And everyone laughed, and surged forward and crowded round.

The fishermen lifted and shook the edges of the net, to stop the little fish from leaping out and make them tumble to the bottom. The woman was nimbler and fiercer than any of the others in this part of the operation. She plucked desperate shrimps from the net and ate them alive. She would have done the same to the interfering children, whom she pushed aside with her hips, shouting: 'Out of the way, whoresons, out of the way, you brats.'

Among the small red mullet, the sardines and the whiting could be seen a spider-fish, the tarantula of the sea, and catching it by the tail she buried it in the sand and crushed it with her feet.

This act of apparent cruelty began to trouble Matteino. He too had abandoned the rope to push to the front of the spectators, and was waiting for his share, when instead he was pushed aside, almost violently, by two fishermen who were carrying, one inside the other, two empty hampers still shiny with scales.

'Mind your backs, mind your backs, make way, *signori*.'

'Out of the way, whoresons.'

'Stay away, brats, understood?'

The net was coming steadily up the beach, growing fatter all the time, its huge mouth with widely separated teeth of cork, and inside a brilliant confusion: it seemed to have scooped up every single treasure in the sea. Even Matteino's friend was no longer sneering; despite the many drag-fishing operations he had witnessed, he had never seen one as abundant as this.

Twisting and turning themselves, with frenzied urgency the fishermen reached inside the net and shook. And at the bottom the fish piled up, and the pile grew and grew, as if the creatures' desperation made them multiply of their own accord.

The first large hamper, carried by two fishermen and emptied on to the sand with truly amazing speed, drew a cry of admiration from the crowd. One had the impression a lightning strike had hit the beach and was fizzing there, held down by a force greater than its own; then another hamper, another, and still more. The fishermen were now laughing like drunkards; the sandy woman had snatched the scarf from her head to fill it with fish.

On the beach, encircled by the almost dazed spectators, the glistening pile was spreading and shimmering, as if made of mercury, and the sight and sound of the smaller fish leaping and flapping against each other in their death throes reminded one of the leaping and crackling of a fire.

The whole tumultuous splendour of the sea seemed to have been tipped out on the shore, and the sea lay quiet as if diminished by it.

Then Matteino thought the moment had come to claim the reward for his efforts. Already other boys were helping themselves to the fish left here and there, and making off as nimbly as grown-up thieves. He had already taken off his bathing cap, loosened the elastic and was beginning to throw in little handfuls of tiny fish that slipped between his fingers like pins.

He could already see his mother's smiling face, her beautiful sea-green eyes were already looking up at him from the bottom of the bathing cap. But he also felt the stinging slap of his father.

'Idle vagabond, son of a dog, keep your hands off things that don't belong to you.'

These jarring words were accompanied by a smack on the head compared to which those his father sometimes gave him were mere caresses. It was the sandy woman who had administered it; and he was obliged to flee on all fours through the legs of the spectators, exactly like a son of a dog, with his cap between his teeth, to escape the woman's fury.

THE CYPRESS

A young cypress tree used to grow hard by the wall dividing our kitchen garden from the neighbour's.

This neighbour was the most steady and methodical man in the district. Although he was well off, he was an employee of the local council, and four times a day I would see him go past, when he went to and from his office, so regularly that you could tell the time by him; even the seasons were recognisable from his clothes, black in winter, grey in spring and autumn and a yellow the shade of straw in the summer.

As to his face, to tell the truth, I don't know: I know that he was often spoken about at home, with an admiration faintly seasoned with irony and envy, pointed out as the perfect example of a normal man, quiet, with no vices: for this reason he did not interest me.

He interested me only when, from time to time, he went

hunting: because he was a famous hunter of wild boar, mouflon and deer.

Then the other keen hunters came to fetch him, men who were not even his friends nor friends with each other, but every so often they gathered in armed bands as if to go off to war.

The whole street sprang to life with a medley of voices, stamping horses, barking and leaping dogs, and a fierce joy filled the air: and it brought me to tears of deep and epic emotion, with my school book in my hand, in the meagre shade of the cypress that grew in the kitchen garden.

"When from an airy hill-top…" for already the dazzling veil of literature was floating between my fantasies and reality. And even our lanky next-door neighbour, on his hunting horse which also served to turn the mill stone for the olive press, became a hero.

Everyone has a touch of the visionary in them at that age; and the deepest passions, the ones that have their roots in the ground but tend towards the infinite, are uniquely the experience of adolescence.

Ambitiousness was my great thing at that time: to become great, to conquer the world. What this conquest amounted to I did not know and still do not. And the presumed greatness was already tinged with sorrow at the mere thought of one day having to give up the solitude and silence that revealed to the troubled soul, by rousing it, the only reason for its existence: a love for things eternal. The finest hours of the day I spent beneath the young cypress. Escaping the oppression of the wall in which its trunk was virtually embedded, it rose towards the open sky in the east, as light as an oversized spindle with its cloud of dark green silk from which I would spin an endless skein of dreams.

I had built a little seat beside the trunk and there I sat at peace. And the tree lived with me, side by side, breathing the same air, growing with me. And naturally I loved the sense of self that being with the tree gave me, my things, both internal and material, that I carried with me into the refuge of its shade and which its shade made even more mine. To begin with it was toys, then school books, then pieces of embroidery, which I believe women are made to learn to distract them from their worries, from both those worries and life's first and greatest revelations.

All the romantic notions of adolescence attached themselves like tendrils of ivy to the tree that was my friend: the first poems were addressed to it; in the greenish light of dusk, the moon and the brilliant stars of the island nights seemed to spring from it; and the song of the nightingale was its own song.

And I hoped to be buried in its shade; but the thought of death did not obscure the thought of life, for in the meantime that shade was the ideal place for secretly reading my first love letters.

The years passed however and the tree of dreams remained sterile. The small things were like the eternal things: they never changed; and that gave a sense of death.

Only the tree grew, with a robust vigour that made it seem destined to reach as high as the stars.

In the afternoons, its shadow fell over the whole of our neighbour's vegetable garden, and affected his cauliflowers which had a truly deathly pallor. A funereal shadow seemed to hang, in any case, over everything and everyone, even the next-door neighbour — who had become even thinner and seemed afraid of his loneliness — and over his damp and silent house. And also over that part of our own kitchen garden that seemed to be shrinking and reverting to wilderness; and on the ageing house; and over me who could see the best years of my girlhood vanish with nothing to show for them.

The same passing of our neighbour under our window, that slow passing and re-passing, at the same hours of the day, as undifferentiated as the passing of the hand over the numbers on the clock-face, filled me with a sense of death. And my mind went to sleep, it curled up on itself, sluggish and resigned and perhaps even happy in its slumbering, like the cat coiled into itself on the warm stone of the roadway.

One single extraordinary event occurred during the last winter I spent at home. A cousin of mine got married, and it fell to another cousin and me to accompany her as maids of honour.

In the procession, alive with colours, velvets, brocades, there was also our next-door neighbour. Dressed in black, taller than anyone else, he reminded me of the cypress tree rising over the flowering kitchen garden.

Yet he was one of the most animated people in the company. He played the guitar and sang. To me it seemed he was doing it only to draw a laugh from the girls who listened to his little love songs.

At the wedding feast I found myself sitting next to him. And I would have remained as indifferent as always if he had not, without turning to look at me, begun to speak to me in a very low voice as if he were speaking to himself.

134

And with horror I learned that he knew everything about me: my age, my habits, my ambitious dreams, my resigned despair at being unable ever to realise them.

'But who told you all this?'

'Who? Your friend.'

'I don't have friends.'

'You have one that you would do well to break away from.'

'I don't understand.'

'Well I understand very clearly. You have one who is causing you to waste your time to no profit, and which is casting a shadow over me as well.'

'Oh! The cypress!'

'The cypress, exactly.'

He poured himself a drink, without looking at me. I saw his hairy white hand open like the paw of a cat when it seizes its prey. He clutched the full glass, emptied it, returned it to the table with something of a bang, with angry decision.

'Cut the cypress down,' he said, without raising his voice. 'It annoys my mother to have to look at it as well. She's always saying: while that tree is there no life will enter our house, nor theirs either. I would like to see my mother die happy; she has worked hard all her life and now she is old. And we are growing older, you and I, *signorina*, I can tell you. What is to be done? Cut the cypress down and let's remove the wall that divides us.'

'Did you understand what I said?' he asked after a moment, during which he seemed to be registering with his fine hunter's hearing the beating of my heart.

But I made no response, other than those pounding heart

beats; and he was too shrewd a man not to interpret them.

And from that moment on I felt I had an enemy living next to me.

More than his, the enmity of his mother began to give me cause for thought.

I knew the mother even less well than the son, even if only a wall separated our two houses. She only left hers twice a year, to go and fulfil her Easter obligations and to purchase, at the best shop in town, fabrics and cloth, everything she would need for the whole year. If she went out a third time, said her mocking and gossipy maids, it would be in search of someone prepared to marry her son.

And now, on this fine February day, the first fine day after the long and sinister winter, while I am standing at the window making love to the sun, I see the neighbours' door open and the old woman come out.

She was tall and dried-out like her son, dressed in black wool and velvet, with the slashed sleeves and the bodice puffed out by a dazzling white blouse. And she too reminded me of the tree, when it is partly covered with snow.

And at her first step I ask myself at lightning speed where on earth she could be going; at the second I reply that Easter is still a long way off; and at the third that it is too soon to be doing her shopping. At the fourth I go pale and my heart stops just as the old woman stops outside our door.

She was coming to ask for my ruin, my death.

Because, after all, the son was an ideal match, and the girls might laugh at his little love songs but they would not refuse him for a husband.

And I wait to be called down to receive the terrible old woman. Minutes pass. No one calls me. I think I must have been the victim of an hallucination. But no, this is the way things are done. The girl must not be present at the asking for her hand in matrimony; she is only summoned afterwards. She must then respond calmly, judiciously, even if the marriage offer is ideal in every respect, in order to preserve the forms.

In fact I see the old woman go away, and when I go down I observe that everybody is wearing a gloomy expression, as if their illusions have been shattered. I do not speak, I wait, sniffing the air, where the old woman seems to have left behind her a smell of sadness. Finally, in the evening, when we are all gathered round the table as if for a family conference, I learn the secret. The old woman has come to ask for the cypress to be cut down.

We discuss it. Some side with the neighbours, sharing their antipathy towards the cypress, others oppose them on the grounds that the neighbours' behaviour is a sudden act of unnecessary arrogance. The neighbours, it is true, are supported by the law which imposes even on plants the duty to keep a reasonable distance from adjoining property. But why have they remembered this law only now?

I know why. And I go out into the garden to greet my friend, whose fate and my own really are united by an invisible thread now. The tree, however, appears strangely cheerful at the news. The night is still chilly but already infused with the pure fragrance of new daffodils; the pearly halo surrounding it seems to emanate from its own branches as they stretch towards the sky; and slowly becoming fuller over its tip shines the bright flame of the moon which transforms it into a miraculous candelabra.

I lean my head against its trunk, to gather strength and advice from it; and it tells me to stay silent, to resist and to wait.

The man, too, from the other side of the dividing wall, was keeping silent and waiting. I could sense him waiting, hidden, with brutal patience as when he lay in ambush among the mastic trees waiting for the happy mountain fawns.

But I was not the happy, because ignorant, mountain fawn, and he knew it. And he enjoyed this kind of hunting, aiming at the cypress because he knew that beneath the cypress bark circulated the blood of my dreams: it was a matter of pride, to preserve himself against a refusal. A matter of pride, and also perhaps a case of romantic whimsy. And after all, is pride, in certain circumstances, not a form of romantic whimsy?

He wanted to protect his standing in the eyes of other women, and also of the men and above all of his mother who considered him a great man. Even if she knew the secret that lay behind this game she lent herself to it with dignity and energy.

And here she is, a fortnight later, back at our door; still dressed in her best as if ready to receive the response to an offer of marriage.

I was waiting for her, with terror, with hatred and with courage. This time I go downstairs without being called, and it is I who receive her, with a cold and bitter courtesy that instantly informs her she is dealing with an adversary worthy of her.

I am the one who interrogates her.

'But why do you want the tree cut down? What harm is it doing to you?'

'It makes the kitchen garden dark and dank. It prevents the vegetables from growing.'

'But why do you need a couple of cabbages, when you are the richest people in town, full of pride, and all the hiding places in your house are stuffed with money?'

She smiles, flattered, instinctively bringing her hand to her bosom, as was her habit anyway, because she really had stowed away a small fortune.

'Money counts for nothing, my girl. What counts is the sun above us, happiness, people. And not even my nieces' children come to play in my kitchen garden any more because they are afraid of catching a chill, with that deathly shadow looming over them.'

'So much the worse for them. You mean they are neither strong nor intelligent children.'

Did she understand? I couldn't say. I know that she stared at me with her large and still very clear eyes; she stared at me as if from the depths of a mirror, with a deceptive expression of indulgence.

'My grandchildren are both strong and intelligent, and God willing, they too will study and go far. The boys, that is, because women must stay at home, their job is to work, to love their family, to make beautiful children and enjoy in peace the blessings God sends us. Happiness lies inside the home.'

I make no reply. What is the point? She too understands that we need to return to the main issue.

'This tree, I'm telling the truth, has always made me sad. It is the tree of the dead, after all. The seed must have been blown over from the cemetery; and it brings misfortune. I'd say cut it down, but in fairness, by common consent, and let's have a fine bonfire the night of Saint John's festival.'

'Why haven't you thought of it earlier?'

'Why would I? It's only when you're very old that you have certain superstitious fears and think about death.'

Ah, I think, and now that you are afraid of dying you want to instal me in your place, to leave the house three times a year, and for the rest of interminable time watch over your useless treasure?

'I am young, and I do not have superstitious fears; and I want to live, and to possess the world,' I tell her in a powerful voice, so powerful that, comically, she puts her hands up to protect her ears. 'We shall not cut the cypress down, no, because I like it. To me, you see, it is more like the tree of good fortune, and I want to keep it.'

'That's all very well,' she said, lowering her voice. 'But do you know the law?'

'I make the law.'

She did not answer. She stood up, unfolding herself very slowly, as though to let me see how tall she was. She was tall, yes, compared with my own small stature, and rigid and strong, hardened by age. She only needed to be holding in her hands a civil code and she could have been a representative of the law.

A month later the bailiff came with the officially stamped document that sought the death of the tree.

It was at this juncture that everyone in the house found themselves in agreement that the demand should be resisted.

There consequently began the lawsuit, the lawyers to start with, then the deputy magistrate and the clerks of the court came to inspect the site.

The tree was enjoying itself in the soft spring that filled out and brightened its stern foliage. It had never been so luxuriant; and then that smell of juniper. The one who suffered was me and at times I grew annoyed at its impassiveness.

If its fate was decided, at least make it happen soon! The sentence was delayed, the hearings were repeatedly postponed.

Only in September did the magistrate pronounce sentence that within a period of thirty days the tree must be felled.

Then a carpenter approached us with an offer to buy the wood and put down the anticipated sum in advance.

In order not to witness the crime I took a desperate decision: to go away, for a while, to some city. And for me it was like the voyage of someone who, to forget a love affair, arranges a highly perilous expedition to hitherto unexplored lands.

I remember the evening of our farewell. The sky already had the greenish transparency of winter, with coppery clouds, gleaming and chilly. There stood the tree, leaning against the wall in a curious state of relaxation, like a man sleeping on his feet, his back against the stones.

And I went to stand beneath it, crying for the dead past, but participating in this act of abandoning something to the infinite, as when beneath the cypresses of cemeteries the sorrow for our dead finds relief in the thought of eternity.

And it was during that short voyage, whose expenses were partly paid out of the money received for the cypress, that all my dreams came to pass, were turned into reality: love, fame, life in a great city; and all the streets of the world opened out like a sunburst around me.

From the 1923 collection *The Flute in the Woods (Il flauto nel bosco)*

La Madre (The Woman and the Priest) by Grazia Deledda

'The syntax of *La Madre* is uncomplicated, but its descriptions are vivid and moving. As with the reeds and the wind, Deledda draws on elements from everyday surroundings to conjure exquisitely lyrical metaphors: "little by little desire crept into that love of theirs, chaste and pure as a pool of still water beneath a wall that suddenly crumbles and falls in ruin". The theme of the priest's forbidden love is rendered more complex by the towering figure of the mother, and the acute psychological strain provoked in each of the protagonists is superbly portrayed by means of analepses, reminiscences, inner questioning and dreams. This allows for the motives to be viewed from each character's perspective, shifting the reader's sympathy in the course of the novel. It can also lead to opposing evaluation on the reader's part. For the author of *Sons and Lovers*, for example, the mother "succeeds, by her old barbaric maternal power over her son, in finally killing his sex life too". For Steegman, "while she is inexorable with the priest her heart yearns over the young man, tender with his grief", and thus "claims the reader's whole sympathy".'

Vilma de Gasperin in *The Times Literary Supplement*

£8.99   ISBN   978 1 912868 63 6   138p   B. Format

The Queen of Darkness (and other stories)
by Grazia Deledda

The ancient traditions of Sardinia feature heavily in this early collection. The stories collected in *The Queen of Darkness*, published in 1902 shortly after Deledda's marriage and move to Rome, reflect her transformation from little-known regional writer to an increasingly fêted and successful mainstream author.

The two miniature psycho-dramas that open the collection are followed by stories of Sardinian life in the remote hills around her home town of Nuoro. The stark but beautiful countryside is a backdrop to the passions, misadventures and injustices which shape the lives of its rugged but all too human inhabitants.

£8.99   ISBN 978 1 915568 15 1   140p   B. Format